SOMETHING STINKS!

For further information, contact:
Tumblehome Learning, Inc.
P.O. Box 171386
Boston, MA 02117, USA
http://www.tumblehomelearning.com

Library of Congress Control Number: 2013939218

Hedrick, Gail E.
SOMETHING STINKS! / Gail E. Hedrick -1st ed, 2nd print

ISBN 978-0-9850008-9-9
1. Children - Fiction 2. Science Fiction 3. Mystery

Cover art/design: Tianxia Xu

Printed in Taiwan

10 9 8 7 6 5 4 3 2 1

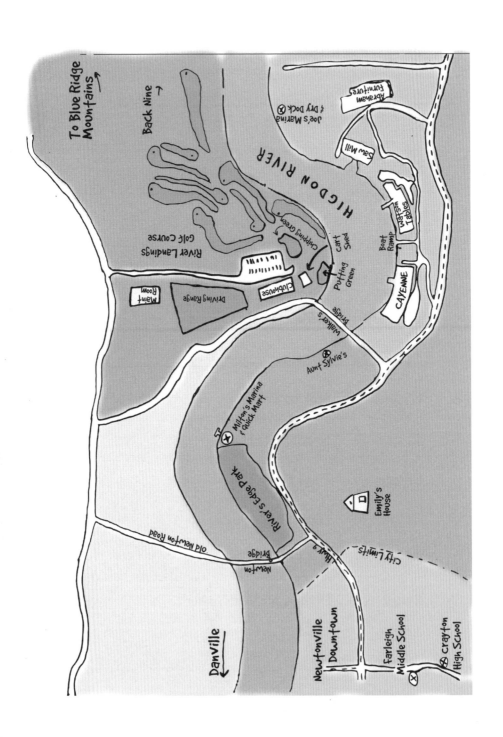

CHAPTER 1
SUMMER NO MORE

The moment I stepped out of Mom's car I knew something was terribly wrong. I gasped as a horrible smell streamed up my nose. It was like that awful mix of odors that drift out of a dumpster behind a bad restaurant. The only problem was I was not behind a bad restaurant. I was at my aunt and uncle's apple orchard. "This is nasty!" I blurted out, and I pinched my nostrils shut.

Aunt Sylvie came bustling out the back door of their little wood-sided cottage, with a handkerchief over her mouth and nose. "Hello, Emily. Best keep holding your breath!"

Mom hauled my little brother Ben out of his seat. She blinked her eyes several times. "Sylvie, what is it?"

"You'll see, it's the worst one yet." Aunt Sylvie beckoned. "Come on."

We followed her around the house, past tidy flower beds filled with late-summer daylilies and mums, and down the grass-covered hill toward the Higdon River. Dead fish, with their bodies bloated and eyes bulging, lay scattered everywhere. Catfish, perch, bluegills, and bass were strewn along the bank and in the water. Some bobbed silently under the wooden dock. "Gosh, Aunt Sylvie," I said, choking. "How many are there?"

"Hundreds," said Uncle Joe, coming up the riverbank carrying a shovel. He wiped his forehead with a red bandanna. "I'm trying to bury 'em to keep the smell down."

"Mommy, stinky fish," said Ben, wrinkling his nose.

"I know," said Mom, nodding. "What's going on here?"

Aunt Sylvie bit her lip. "We don't know, but it's happened before. I think the last time was early in the summer, right after y'all left."

We'd just returned home to Southwest Virginia from spending the entire summer over in Tennessee. It wasn't the way I would have picked to spend my time before starting seventh grade but no one asked me. My dad's a project manager for a regional utility company, and since *he'd* had to go, he was sure my mom, little brother, and I would love to tag along. I didn't get to sleep in my own bed for months, had to spend endless hours of "quality time" with a three-year-old, and constantly wondered what my friends were doing back home. Now, this. What would kill so many fish in this perfect little river?

Aunt Sylvie patted Ben on the head and went on. "We reported that first one to the county back then, but nobody seemed too concerned. Later we heard someone in the office had accidentally deleted the call log for that day."

Uncle Joe grumbled, "We called again yesterday when we started seeing a few dead ones here and there. This time some inspector came out and tromped all around. He glanced at the water but didn't test it. He said everyone always wants to blame the big companies upstream for these sorts of things, but the factories have 'state regulations' they have to follow. Unlike the farmers."

He jammed the shovel into the squishy red clay. "That was when the guy seemed to turn on me asking what kind of pesticides I used. I told him we're organic growers. I use soap and water and nothing else. He laughed and said it must be some kind of potent suds to get this result. That's when I showed him the door."

"He sounds like a jerk," I said. "What are they going to do about it?"

Uncle Joe shook his head. "They just sent us a status report stamped *Incident submitted - necessity for further action inconclusive*."

"What does that mean?" I asked.

"It means he's not going to do anything. Case closed."

Mom said, "That's ridiculous."

"It is," Uncle Joe agreed. "But it appears we're on our own, so we'll deal with it."

Mom surveyed the scene. "Listen, I have to get to the pharmacy before it closes. How about I have John come out to help you clean up?"

Uncle Joe chuckled. "Your husband doesn't need to lose a day's pay to bury fish."

"We'll be fine," said Aunt Sylvie, pulling her apron strings tight around her waist. "I'll be out here in a few minutes with my barn boots on and my own shovel."

I looked at the bodies clumping against my uncle's little fishing boat and bobbing ashore, pushed by the river currents. The creepy combination of the smell and sight of these fish made me want to run away and never come back. I glanced at my sweet aunt and uncle. Their shoulders sagged with either defeat or exhaustion; I didn't know which. It was awful to see them like this. I sighed. "Mom, you take Ben and leave me here to help."

"What about getting your school supplies?"

"We can go after you get Ben's medicine. My list isn't that huge, so we can go after you come back."

"Okay, plan the rest of my day," said Mom, grinning. "What about Leanne?"

My best friend and I had shopped together for school supplies forever. "Oh, shoot. I'll need to let her know, but I bet she won't mind going later. When I tell her what the problem is, she'll understand. She loves it out here, too."

"Oh, you dear child," said Aunt Sylvie, giving me a hug. Then she peered up at me. "When did you get so tall?"

"Everyone looks gigantic to you, Aunt Sylvie. I'm still right at 5'5"."

"Well, maybe it's that new short hairdo. It shows off your natural curl. Now, I need to find you some gloves and a rake. Jenny, bring little Ben and on your way to the car I'll get you some cider to take along for later."

I wished it was later and all this mess was already bagged up. As the others walked away, I turned toward the river and Uncle Joe, but all I could see were the fish. Their eyes were getting to me and the usually crisp air out here seemed as rotten as the inside of a sewer. "This is so sad. My favorite place in the whole world is a graveyard. How could something like this happen? Why can't something great ever stay that way?"

"Well, it's looking like we might never know," said Uncle Joe. "Hopefully, it won't be like this the next time you're here. By the way, what did you say about your side-kick, Leanne?"

"Oh, I've gotta call her. I guess I should've gone up to the house to use the phone."

"Shoot, no," said Uncle Joe, "use my cell phone. I'm surprised you don't have one of these gizmos."

"Tell that to my parents, please," I said, entering the phone number of my best friend since kindergarten.

"Leanne? Hi, we're going to be kind of late. We're out at my aunt and uncle's place. You won't believe what a mess..." I listened for a moment, not believing my ears. I said, "I thought you wanted to go."

I listened a moment, wishing I had the power to change what Leanne was saying. "Well, okay, if that's what you want to do." I clicked the button on the phone to 'end' and stood facing away from Uncle Joe, hoping I wouldn't cry. How dumb for a stupid phone call to matter this much.

I sighed and turned around. "I haven't seen Leanne all summer. We were supposed to go school shopping together today just like every year. Mom always takes us and we stop for milkshakes at the Dairy Barn on the way home. Sounds corny, I know."

Uncle Joe took off his hat and scratched his head. "Nope, it sounds like a nice plan. So, what happened?"

"She bailed on me to go shopping with this fancy, rich girl, Cynthia Craver. And instead of milkshakes, she's going to Cyn's country club for dinner."

"Hard to compete with that," said Uncle Joe.

"Tell me about it," I agreed. "I left here having an amazing best friend. And now, who knows?"

Uncle Joe replaced his hat. "Well, I'm sorry that happened. And I'm sorry we won't see Leanne. I've missed her."

"Me too." Yup, my besty ditched me, so for the second time today I wondered, why can't something great ever stay that way?

CHAPTER 2
TOO MUCH RACQUET

Early Sunday afternoon, I sat at the kitchen table organizing my backpack, stashing new pens, colored pencils and notebooks in the various pockets, and eyeing the clock. When the phone rang, Mom grabbed it as she was expecting a call from a member of her garden club. She listened a moment, then waved the phone at me. "It's Leanne, something about this afternoon."

I held my breath, not wanting to be dumped again. Then I took the phone. "Let me guess, no tennis."

"You are so wrong, Miss Jump-to-Conclusions. I had some chores to finish."

"You still do chores? I thought maybe Cyn's family loaned you their maid."

"Oh, please. I'm the only maid this house will ever see," said Leanne. "So, I can do tennis, but I have to bring Beth."

"No," I complained. "No little sisters."

Leanne sighed. "It's that or not play. My mom's going to visit someone in the hospital, so I've got to babysit. If you bring Ben, we can park them in the sandbox."

I made a face. "Okay, but we won't get to play much tennis."

"Stop whining, girl," said Leanne giggling. "It won't be so bad."

Later, as I pedaled along, I thought, it won't be so good either. I was riding Mom's bike, complete with baby seat. With Ben's added weight, plus the tennis bag, I wobbled all over the road. Still, I had it easy compared to Leanne. As we met near the park entrance, I said, "Whoa, what a load."

Leanne grinned. "Toys, snacks, and extra diapers!"

There was something else different about her. I stared at Leanne. "Um, are you wearing a *tennis outfit*? Where did that come from?"

"You love it, right?" Leanne asked, as she put down the kickstand and stepped gracefully off the bike. She twirled so the pale-pink skirt flared out almost as far as her long blond hair. "Cynthia's dad, you know, Mr. Craver? Anyway, he runs the Cayenne sportswear factory. It's been around forever, but they've just started an athletic line. You know which factory I'm talking about?"

I nodded. Our town is known as the sweatshirt capital of the world. People come from all over to buy jogging suits and T-shirts at our factory outlets. I guess every town has to be famous for something. Why not sweatshirts?

Leanne gushed on. "The factory's been around forever, but they just started a new tennis line. And *I'm* the same size as the samples. He gave me this whole outfit! Do you believe that?"

I looked down at my cutoffs, then tapped my faded orange UVA visor, which I had slid on at the last second. Wearing this, I probably looked like a curly redheaded boy. "Guess I'm underdressed."

"Nah," said Leanne, unpacking the stuff for the little kids, "you look normal. Love your tennis shoes. Besides, we're at the park, not the club."

"Oh, yeah, Miss Country Club."

Leanne giggled. "That place is so neat. Mr. Craver is letting me take golf lessons with Cynthia. She has her own clubs and has taken lessons for years. Funny, she's still not very good, but the golf pro says I have 'potential'."

"I didn't know you liked golf," I said, as we settled the kids in the sandbox.

"I didn't know I liked golf either till I tried it." Leanne swung her racquet. "It's something different. You're doing new stuff, too. Aren't you learning guitar?"

"I took a class this summer. I can play, like, three songs. But basically, I'm just the same old Emily. I like things just the way they've always been."

"I was like that, too," agreed Leanne, "but since my parents split up, nothing is like it used to be."

"Oh, I'm such an idiot," I said, tapping my head. "I keep forgetting your dad left. It's like he should still be here with his car in your driveway." I realized I had no idea what Leanne's life was like now. My dad was home every night, and though my parents sometimes argued over things like where they should have dinner or what color to paint the house, they were basically a ridiculously happy couple. "Is it awful?"

"It was for a while. You left town, then he left us. My mom and I walked around like zombies. She'd forget to feed us and I'd just sit on my bed."

"Wow, why didn't you tell me all this when I called you?"

"I actually wrote you a couple of e-mails, then deleted them. I couldn't talk about it for the first couple of months. It was just so icky. I kept hoping they'd made a horrible mistake and things would go back to like they used to be." Leanne shrugged. "That never happened, but it's a little better now. I finally got busy doing stuff. And Mom's stopped crying every five seconds."

It's no fun seeing one of your parents cry. You don't know whether to hug them, do something silly to make them laugh, or just leave them alone. I hadn't had the most exciting summer on record, but at least my parents didn't get divorced. "So, I'm sorry about everything, but I'm glad it's better. Um, should we play?"

"Yup," said Leanne, spinning her racquet. "And, if you liked things the way they used to be, then I'm going to win, like always. Serve it up!"

We went at each other, playing as hard as if we were in a tournament. We had each won a set when I called for time out. "I need a drink."

"So, you're not just throwing in the towel?" said Leanne, trotting to the net. "Did you lose weight this summer?"

"Maybe a little. I swam a lot of laps and lifted weights some."

"I knew something was different." She pointed to the kids. "They're doing pretty good. Let's keep that going and pass out the snacks."

"Good idea, and we can drink some... Uh oh," I said, smacking my forehead. "I meant to bring some of Aunt Sylvie's cider."

"Oh, Em, you had cider and didn't bring any?" Leanne gave the kids some crackers.

"I just forgot, with having to bring Ben and all." I gulped some water from the water fountain. "It was a weird trip out to the orchard. The whole place smelled awful."

"That cute little cabin? To me, it always has the aroma of chocolate chip cookies."

"Not on Tuesday. Bunches of dead fish had washed up as far as you could see along both sides of the riverbank. Guts were showing, eyes bulging. It was so gross."

Leanne wrinkled her sun-pinked nose. "Frankly, I think fish are kind of stinky even when they're alive."

I shook my head, remembering the sight. "You really had to be there to appreciate how bad it was."

"Sounds disgusting."

"Apparently the county guy, who never even tested the water, tried to blame those hundreds of dead fish on my uncle's apple orchard."

"He thought your uncle killed the fish?"

"Yeah, like maybe he'd dumped pesticides into the river. The thing is, Uncle Joe doesn't use pesticides—never has."

"I wonder how it happened," said Leanne.

"I don't know but I'm gonna find out. Do you want to help me?"

Leanne shrugged. "I guess, if I have time. I'm really busy with..."

The sound of a car horn filled the air. Not the usual honking sound, but the musical kind. This car horn blared "You Are My Sunshine" and came from the white Cadillac pulling into the parking lot. The convertible top was down and the man at the wheel wore a big, white cowboy hat. Standing in the back, waving like someone in the Pumpkin Parade, stood Cynthia Craver.

"What's she doing here?"

"I don't know," said Leanne, waving back. "I *did* tell her we were playing tennis, but I didn't tell her where."

"Where else would we be? Neither of us belongs to any private tennis clubs." I picked up my racquet. "Come on, let's finish our match."

Leanne glanced at Cynthia, as she stepped out of the car. "Um, in a minute. I'd better see what she wants. It'll take just a sec."

Before Leanne could move, the Cadillac pulled away and Cynthia ran across the parking lot to our court. First, she patted Beth on the head, poked Ben in his chubby tummy, nodded at me, and then gushed to Leanne, "Look what Daddy just got! These are the latest racquets from Pro Strokes. They send him stuff all the time because they like to have their equipment in the ads with our clothes. They just finished using these in a new commercial and Daddy said we could have them to play with. Come on, Leanne, let's go."

Leanne fingered the racquet. The frame glistened with a sky-blue metallic finish. "Wow, it's light as a feather."

Cynthia bragged, "It's a J11X. My daddy says they'll sell for hundreds of dollars when they go on the market It's a 'winner's' racquet."

I sniffed and said, "It looks nice, but sometimes these old trusty models do just as well."

Leanne glanced at our scuffed wood racquets, and then back at the J11X. "Em, do you mind?"

I did mind and should have told her, but expecting Leanne to remember that best friends always stick together, I shrugged.

Leanne shrugged right back and pointed the racquet toward the court. "Yeah, I should test it out. We won't be long."

Stunned by her remark, I knelt down and pretended to fuss with my shoelace. I didn't want either one of them to see my watery eyes.

"Thanks, and Em, since you're going to be here anyway," said Leanne, nudging the diaper bag in my direction, "Beth is probably due for a change."

CHAPTER 3
DOORS, DOORS, AND MORE DOORS

Monday after school, I peered into the refrigerator. "May I have the last soft drink?"

"Sure," said Mom, coming up from the basement carrying the laundry basket. "Did school improve your mood?"

"School was just school." I took a long swig from the soda can and sighed. "Honestly, I didn't think anyone noticed I was a little grumpy."

"Well, you were hard to ignore," said Mom. "After tennis, you slammed every door in the house you came in contact with. The cabinets, your bedroom, the closets. Do you want to talk about it?"

"There's nothing to talk about. Leanne is way different. Plus, she has a new best friend with lots of money and breasts!"

"Ouch, that's a tough combination," said Mom, giving my shoulder a squeeze. "Don't worry, you're starting to develop, too."

I looked down at the tiny bumps on my chest. "You have a great imagination."

"Oh, hush," said Mom. "Listen, Leanne had a heartbreaking summer. Did she talk about it?"

"Yeah, a little," I agreed. "When her parents split up, her dad moved to Aspen. Then her mom bought the hair salon she worked for, which I guess is nice, but now she works all the time."

"That's got to be hard," agreed Mom. "This thing with Cynthia could just be a carryover from the past few months. You said they met in summer school?"

I nodded. "I guess Cynthia's always gone to Chatham Hill for their big deal music program. But, apparently she got tired of practicing the flute or whatever and her parents are making her try public school. Lucky for me, huh?"

"Unfortunately, no. However, Leanne needed somebody and she found Cynthia. Now it kind of sounds like she's been swept along by the whole Craver family."

"Yup, and I can't compete with the Cravers. I don't know what to do about it."

"Well," said Mom, "You've got a couple of choices. One would be to make some new friends."

I stared at Mom. "There are no girls at my school this year that seem remotely interesting. They're all giggly and spend all day talking about boys and makeup." I shuddered.

Mom nodded. "Okay, then I guess you'll have to go with your second option and just keep trying with Leanne."

"I asked her to help me find out what caused the big fish mess out at Aunt Sylvie's. She said she might and we could figure out a plan."

Mom smiled. "That sounds promising."

"Right," I said, thinking. "Maybe she'd want to sleep over Friday."

"Good idea," answered Mom. "See if she wants to come for supper, too."

Changing clothes after PE the next day, I stopped Leanne in the locker room. "Hey, do you want to eat with us Friday and then spend the night?"

"Sure," said Leanne. "Mom just gave me a whole bunch of new nail polish samples. We can try them all."

Was she crazy? The Leanne I knew hardly ever wore lip gloss, let alone nail polish. I was about to burst out laughing thinking how polish would look on my clipped short, stubby fingernails when Cynthia Craver came around the lockers. She ran a hand through her mass of chocolate-colored curls and said, "If you two are making plans for Friday night, make sure you allow for us going to the flea market after school. There's no telling how long we'll be."

Leanne snapped her fingers, and said "Oh, my gosh, I forgot about the flea market."

I blinked my eyes. "The flea market? You hate that place!"

"Not since she's into antiques," Cynthia said.

"Into *what*?" I asked, not believing what I had heard.

"Antiques," said Cynthia, nudging Leanne. "According to my mama, Leanne has a good eye for decorating, so she's helping us check out all the antique stalls to get the perfect accessories for our new house."

"And don't forget these," said Leanne, shaking her wrists, loaded with bracelets.

"Ooh, yeah," nodded Cynthia, holding her arm out. "See all these cool old bangles?"

I nodded and kept getting dressed. The bracelets looked like rainbows on their wrists.

Cynthia went on. "We've been collecting these vintage bracelets all summer. They're the hottest thing in all the fashion magazines."

"Really?" I ran a comb through my hair and slipped on my tiny amethyst ring. "I don't read many magazines."

Cynthia watched Leanne head toward the hair dryers. As soon as Leanne turned one on, Cynthia pivoted toward me and jingled her bracelets. "Leanne's told me stuff about you. She mentioned you're not into fashion. I can see she's right."

My eyes stung. I tried a fast joke. "Yeah, my fashion statement is my PE uniform." I grabbed my stuff and flounced out of the locker room with as much dignity as I could suck up. It didn't last long. As soon as I got out to the empty hall, the tears of frustration began to roll.

CHAPTER 4
NOW WHAT?

Out in the hall, I rummaged through my book bag, keeping my head down as I walked. Where was a tissue when I needed one? As usual, one appeared at the bottom of the bag, wadded up and stuck to a piece of old chewing gum. Yup, that's just how I felt, thanks to Cynthia, like thrown-away gum.

I sighed, dried the last tear, and stood outside the door to my English class wondering if I was settled down enough to go in. The tardy bell helped me make up my mind. I slid into my seat just as it finished clanging.

"In the nick of time, Miss Sanders," said Mr. Chicelli.

"I know." Usually English was my favorite subject. "Are we doing vocab today?"

"No, Emily," said Mr. Chicelli. "We're starting the year off with a bang—essays!" He smiled at the class as if he were accepting an award.

Everyone groaned, and I muttered, "The end of a perfect day."

"Emily, since you seem out of sorts, maybe a little exercise would do you good," said Mr. Chicelli. "Take this bowl and give each person a slip of paper from it. Everyone will get a different subject. You have forty minutes to write. Begin as soon as you have your topic."

I got the bowl and wandered around the room in a trance, passing out the slips of paper. Finally, when there was only one left, I sat down and opened it. It said, "In 250 words or less, write an essay on a person, living or dead, who has had an impact on your life."

With pen and paper ready, I pondered this assignment. I glanced up at Mr. Chicelli who was busy grading papers. His hair was the same color as that witch's Cynthia Craver. Hah!

Later, Mr. Chicelli broke my concentration. "Emily, you seem to have exceeded the word count." He stood beside my desk, pointing at the sheets of paper I had filled with speed scribbling.

I looked at what I was doing, and shook myself. Wow, I love to write, but words had never spilled out of me like this. "Oops. Sorry, sir."

He peered down at the pages I'd written. "Sounds like something dark."

"Well, I guess I was venting," I agreed. "But it's about a real person."

"All right," he said, tapping my essay. "I'm going to look this over before the bell rings. Please see me after class."

"Okay."

As he walked up the aisle, the boy behind me whispered, "Already in trouble, Em?"

I shook my head, and whispered back. "Very funny."

I didn't want to miss the bus, so as soon as the bell rang, I rushed up to Mr. Chicelli's desk. "You wanted to see me, sir?"

"The essay topics were intended to be fun and inspirational, Miss Sanders. This is bordering on inappropriate."

Rats, that kid behind me was right. First week, I was heading downhill fast. "I'm sorry. It's just that this person has messed up my—"

Mr. Chicelli held up his hand. "That's enough. What I was *also* going to say is you are a good writer. I'd like you to consider writing for the school newspaper."

"I'm not sure. I have swim practice."

"I understand," said Mr. Chicelli, "but we work around all the sports' practice schedules. Plus, you get 10 bonus points per semester added to your English grade."

I stood there thinking there was a distinct possibility I wouldn't be hanging out with Leanne very much. Plus, the ten points wouldn't hurt.

"Sounds good." I grabbed my pen and signed up for the newspaper staff.

Mr. Chicelli nodded, and said "The first meeting is Thursday at 3:30."

After school, Mom met me at our front door, and asked, "Did you talk to Leanne about Friday night?"

I nodded, and said, "Yup, she'll be here, after she gets finished at the flea market with you know who."

"Flea market?" asked Mom, with a surprised tone.

"Go figure." I sighed and trudged toward the kitchen. No matter how bad things seemed, I was always ready for food.

"Well, at least she's coming," said Mom, softly. "Do you have a lot of homework?"

"A little math," I said, looking through the mail. "Oh, one thing. Since I'm basically friendless, and could become bored out of my mind, I signed up to work on the school newspaper. My English teacher is the advisor."

"That's great, Em. You like to write."

I nodded. "I do. Anyway, the first meeting is Thursday, and I already know what my first article will be about." I reached for the phone, dialed a familiar number. "Uncle Joe?"

"Hello there Emily. You home from school already?"

"Yes, sir, I am and I have a favor to ask. When we were out there the other day, you said something about a report the county sent you after the fish died."

"Yup. What a waste of taxpayers' money mailing that thing."

I nodded. "I agree. I want to talk with those people and see if they would consent to an interview. I'm on the school newspaper staff this year."

"Wish you luck. I don't know if this is interview-worthy. I called the Trib. When I told them there hadn't been any more fish wash up since the weekend, the reporter said that wasn't much of a story and he'd pass."

"Yeah, it's weird how it comes and goes. To me, *that's* a story. Oh, well. You'll get me that report?"

"I'll do it today," said Uncle Joe. "I'll just fax it to you."

"Wow, you have a fax machine?"

"Yes, missy. I also have an MP3 player."

"You are kidding!"

"Nope, I listen to tunes while I'm riding the tractor. Sylvie wants one for when she's rolling out pie crusts."

"You two are quite the techies," I said, giggling. "I'll let you know what I dig up about the fish."

"We're grateful for whatever you can do. Bye."

Mom had been listening to me and nodded at the phone. "That's nice of you."

I nodded. "We'll see."

As I hung up, Mom said, "You know, this newspaper thing might be a new friend opportunity."

"I doubt it. Remember, I've known everyone in my school for years."

"Maybe so," said Mom. "Just keep an open mind."

"Mom, stop," I said, shaking my head. Didn't she realize that I'm not the type to just pluck friends out of thin air? I wasn't expecting friends. I just hoped the newspaper staff wouldn't all be geeks, or even worse, annoying troublemakers like Cynthia Craver. One in my life was enough.

CHAPTER 5
NEVER RAISE YOUR HAND

Thursday after school, I headed down the hall toward Mr. Chicelli's room and nearly plowed into Ms. Smith.

"Hi, Emily. How was your summer?"

"Pretty good. We spent some time over in Tennessee."

"That sounds nice. I biked through Maine and then came back to create all new lesson plans. Have you been thinking about your science project?"

I glanced at my watch, trying to think of the best way to answer this question. Ms. Smith's life was all about science projects. I'd learned that last year in her class. "Well, you know I always have trouble deciding what to do. Lucky I've got some time to think about it."

"Well, sure you do. Try to think about something relevant to your life."

I shrugged. "Sorry, but science doesn't seem relevant to anything in my life."

"Hmm, you're on the swim team, right? How about what you eat and how it affects performance? Or, which swim suit offers the least resistance in the water?"

I nodded politely, hearing her but not really listening. I *needed* to get to the newspaper meeting. Hey, wait, did she say relevant? "Ms. Smith, why would fish die in a perfectly nice river?"

Now, Ms. Smith checked *her* watch. "Wow, Emily, that's a big question, because simply put, there are a boatload of possibilities. I need to get to a department meeting. Come by my classroom one day during your study hall, and we'll make a list." She snapped her fingers. "Fish dying? Sounds like a science project premise to me." Ms. Smith whirled around and strode off toward the Faculty Center.

I rushed into Mr. Chicelli's room for the newspaper meeting. "I'm sorry I'm late. I got caught by Ms. Smith."

Mary Carnell said, "Did she ask if you'd picked a science project yet?"

"Always," I replied, and sat beside Mary. "And, big surprise, apparently I might already have picked one."

"Extra-credit diva," whispered Drew.

"Yeah, I probably am," I said, grinning at a fellow seventh-grader I'd known since kindergarten. "It might be nice for once to pick something early so I don't have it hanging over my head."

"Good philosophy, Miss Sanders, so let us continue," said Mr. Chicelli, from the back of the room. "Since most of last year's newspaper staff graduated, we're starting this year with a less-experienced group. We've been discussing the position of editor. Anyone willing to try it?"

Silence.

"Sam?" asked Mr. Chicelli, moving toward his desk. "Are you interested?"

"I'm thinking, sir," answered a tall, deeply tanned boy.

"Well, you did say you'd had newspaper experience at your old school."

"Yeah," said Sam. "I can probably handle it."

"Who is he?" I whispered.

"Eighth-grader, transfer from Greensboro," answered Mary Carnell.

I studied Mary for a minute wondering what the theme of her outfit was. Mary's dad was a famous sculptor and her mom wrote romance novels, both pretty unusual occupations in our small town. Mary's talent was painting, and she was good enough to have her art hanging at the central library community gallery. Last year, she'd occasionally show up wearing all one-color outfits that usually had a theme. Today, the color was orange. Sometimes, the themes were hard to guess, like the day she wore all silky white with sparkly beads and a long fringed scarf. That outfit was to honor Elvis's birthday. "I like your 'celebrating autumn' look," I said, pointing to Mary's sweater. Glancing up at Sam, I whispered, "How did the new guy get such a good suntan?"

"I heard he spent part of the summer with relatives on the California coast."

"Are there any objections?" said Mr. Chicelli, getting everyone's attention. "Well, Sam, it's unanimous. As the new editor, what's your first order of business?"

"Get help," said Sam, shoving his shaggy black hair off his forehead. "I need an assistant editor, sports writers, and a graphics pro."

Four guys raised their hands. Each wanted sports. Sam chose two and assigned the sports each of them would cover. I listened for a moment and asked, "Isn't someone going to cover *girls' sports*?"

"Oh, you mean someone might actually want to read about field hockey and volleyball?" Sam asked. "We can give them a few sentences."

Grumbles echoed from the girls in the room. Mr. Chicelli said, "I hate to intervene, but we should have all sports covered, so you might need one more writer."

"Understood," said Sam, pointing to me. "How about 'Red'?"

"Call me Emily, and I'll consider it."

He bowed, and said, "Thank you, oh gracious one. Now, about the graphics person. Anyone draw?"

I looked around and then said, "I think Mary is the one you need. She's won the county fair art competition for three straight years."

Sam raised his dark eyebrows, and said, "Impressive. Want the job?"

Mary nodded and grinned her thanks to me.

"All right," said Sam, looking around. "Who's gonna be Number Two, the one that does all the hard work and makes me look good?"

Everyone groaned, and Mr. Chicelli said, "Gee, Sam, you're making the spot for assistant editor sound irresistible!"

Then I made a big mistake. I raised my hand. "What do you actually have to do?"

Mr. Chicelli said, "Some writing, like pieces about the school, helping me proofread and edit the articles into newspaper form."

I stared at a scuff on my shoe, and thought for a minute.

Mr. Chicelli waited, and then he said, "You'd be a good assistant editor, Emily."

"Then it's settled," said Sam, giving a thumbs-up sign. "Let's vote."

Everyone's hand shot up, and before I could blink, I was assistant editor to a guy with an ego as big as a bus.

Chapter 6
Stinkin' Fun:
No Fish Allowed

Friday night, I yelled down the stairs, "Mom, any sign of Leanne?"

"For the thousandth time, no," called Mom. "She'll be here soon. Dinner's almost ready and she's never late for my fried chicken."

Just then the doorbell rang, and I sprinted down to answer it. I opened the door to a blast of cool night air, and to Leanne. "Took you long enough."

"I know," said Leanne, nodding. "Cynthia acted like she wanted to hit every booth in the flea market."

"Maybe she wanted to keep you from coming."

"Oh, please, she's not like that," said Leanne, shaking her head.

"Good to know," I muttered, looping Leanne's duffel bag over the stair post. We headed for the kitchen. "Mom, look who smelled chicken."

"Hi, Leanne," Mom said, lifting a squash casserole from the oven. She set it on a hot-pad and threw her arms around Leanne. "We've missed you. I was so sorry to hear about your parents."

Leanne leaned her head on Mom's shoulder. "Thanks. It's been pretty bad."

I thought, *Mom can really be sweet sometimes. I've got to stop being so whiny and remember how torn up Leanne's life has been.*

"I can only imagine," said Mom nodding. "Well, remember we're always here if you need us." She pointed to the dining room. "Now, back to business. Could you two fill the glasses? Emily, I hear your dad coming in, so we're ready. Will someone make sure Ben gets his hands washed?"

Everyone scurried around, doing those last minute things that get a meal on the table, and then we ate. And ate. When Mom said, "Now, who's ready for dessert?" it was obvious to me no one could down even one more green bean.

33

"I'll have to wait," I said, patting my stomach. "I'm so full I could burst."

Leanne nodded. "Me too."

"Okay," said Mom, shooing us from the dining room. "You can come back for pie later."

Dad held up his hand. "Did you see the fax from Uncle Joe?"

I nodded. "Sure did, and I talked to the county guy after school today. He sent a report to Richmond and said he'd let me know if they got a response. And he mentioned some other stuff for me to check out. I might, because it doesn't sound like he's going to do it."

Leanne poked me in the ribs. "Listen to you, all Miss Assistant Editor of the school paper."

"Emily," said Mom, "you didn't tell us. Congratulations!"

"Thanks," I said. "It just happened yesterday. It's no biggie."

"It's something to be proud of," said Dad.

Mom said, "Well, let's let these girls go. I hear they have nail polish to try and hair to style."

"Right," I said, stretching a red curl out from my head. "Like there's much hope for this mop."

"Maybe if we use an entire jar of setting gel," answered Leanne with a giggle. As we headed upstairs, she added, "So, tell me, have you noticed all the cute guys around school this year?"

"Not really. They're just the same ol' guys except some of them grew."

"Yeah, but that transfer kid Sam Wheeler is gorgeous," said Leanne, pretending to bite her knuckles.

When we got to my room, Leanne opened her duffel bag, pulled out a plastic box and flipped the lid open. The inside compartments held a rainbow of different nail polishes. She said, "I'm going Midnight Rose, maybe with some vanilla dots."

Since I had the stubbiest nails on earth, any color would do. I grabbed a random bottle and shook it. "Um, I guess Sam's cute enough if you like really long hair, which I don't."

"Good thing, since he's spoken for. Cynthia met him about a month ago at a pool party. He's been calling her every night since."

"They make the perfect couple," I said, spreading a flash of Coral Sunlight polish across my thumbnail. "Miss Big Chest and Mr. Big Head!"

"Ooh—and here lives 'Miss Jealous'."

"I'm not jealous. It's just that he's the editor for the paper, and like you said, I'm assistant editor. He's already calling me his slave."

"I wouldn't care what he called me," said Leanne with a sigh. "He's impossibly cute and funny. How can you not like him?"

I blew on my nails. "Easy. He's bossy and lazy. He ordered us to come up with five story ideas by Tuesday or else."

"Seriously, how hard can that be?"

Just as I was about to tell her, the telephone rang. I picked up and said, "Hello?" and then tossed the receiver down on the bed. "It's for you. I'll be in the bathroom."

Leanne said, "Hello? Oh, hi, Cynthia. Yeah, I forgot my cell. Anyway, you found me. What's up?"

I stomped down the hall, turned into the bathroom, and paced around in circles. Whipping open the medicine cabinet, I grabbed my toothpaste and brush. I was attacking my plaque when Leanne poked her head in.

"May I?"

Taking a deep breath, and with as much dignity as possible, I spit into the sink. "Come in if you want. Keep in mind there's no *phone* in here."

"Aw, come on, I didn't talk long," said Leanne, tugging me out the door. "Let's see what you can do with my hair."

I shrugged. "Okay, but you know this isn't my best thing." I grabbed some hair pins. Maybe I'll try one of those French twists."

"Try not to stab me."

I sat down on the bed and began to brush her hair. "Anyway, give me some good story ideas."

"Well, I guess there's the obvious boring ones, like something about the new teachers this year. Oh, wait—a cool video game store just opened on Market Street. It's really great and right across the street there's a new cupcake shop. I bet those businesses would love you to write about them. Then, closer to prom season, you can write about my mom's hair salon."

"Okay, sure. These are great ideas. Maybe you should be on the paper."

"Crazy girl, remember what a bad speller I am? Hey, what about a personality article? Like in the Sunday paper, you know, a mover and shaker in the school. Of course, I don't mean someone like that weird Mary Carnell I've seen you with."

I shrugged again. "Mary's okay. She's *different*, but nice."

Leanne burst out laughing, and dove for the bed. When she got herself under control, she said, "Yesterday she was dressed like a jack-o'-lantern. Cynthia says theme dressing is bizarre. Anyway, speaking of Cyn, she's the type of person you should write about."

Was she kidding? As if it wasn't enough Cynthia had stolen my friend, now I had to write about the girl?

Leanne ignored my open-mouthed stare and continued. "Think about it. She's a great dresser, gives very cool parties, and comes from a well-known family. Maybe you could write a monthly column, 'Personality of the Month'. She'd be perfect for the first one."

I remembered my grandmother always said nobody's perfect, which, in my opinion, included Cynthia Craver. "Yeah, well, I guess that's an okay idea. It's just that I wanted to be on the paper to write about important stuff. Like interviewing the school safety officer about bullying, or talking to people about plans for the science fair."

Leanne stared at me. "Important stuff? *Maybe.* Fun to read about? No, that stuff is *boring.*"

"Well, then what about the environment? Kids are interested in that. Remember, I was hoping you would help me do an investigative report about who or what is responsible for killing the fish at Aunt Sylvie's place."

"Do you mean like talk to people and write down what they say? I wouldn't know how to do that."

"Yes, you would—it's not hard. Like today when I talked to the guy who wrote the report for the county about the dead fish. I didn't have to talk to him in person, I just phoned him. So, you could do something like that."

"Maybe."

"Just take notes while the person's talking. Like this guy said there are so many things that can kill fish, I shouldn't waste my time trying to figure it out. But I told him it was important to my family. He said some reports indicate fish die from junk from cat litter factories, waste from chicken farms and fertilizer runoff from golf courses. So, I could try to check out any or all of those things if it was *that* important to me. Then he hung up."

"He sounds like a real prize."

"At least he gave me some ideas," I said. "So, will you help me?"

"Um, do we have cat litter factories here?"

"Nope, and we don't have any chicken farms. So, that's why this might be really easy. That fancy golf club out on the river, River Landings, could be causing all the fish to die."

Leanne stared up at the ceiling and sighed. "That's where I take my golf lesson."

I snapped my fingers. "Perfect, then you know who we should talk to."

Leanne stared at me like I was a little kid who'd stolen a cookie. "I know who we *could* talk to, but I am not getting involved in this. I don't want to tick off the guy who's teaching me to play golf. I don't want to insult Mr. Craver. He's, like, the vice president of the club's board of directors. No, not me."

"I can't believe you're so wimpy about a major issue like this. They could be polluting our river."

Leanne shook her head. "If there was major pollution, people wouldn't be water skiing or letting their dogs swim out there. All you've got is a few stinky fish. That's it. Dead fish? I think you spent too much time swimming in that condo pool this summer. You've waterlogged your brain. Think of fun things to write about, like makeup or shoes. Or fun hobbies like skateboarding. Did I say *fun*?"

"You did, several times," I said, looking away to hide my disappointment. Even though we were only sitting two feet apart, the distance between us seemed wide as a river.

CHAPTER 7
WHAT'S THE <u>REAL</u> STORY?

After school Monday, I rushed into Mr. Chicelli's room, late from having to pick up a swim team practice schedule. I shoved it and a little blue plastic box into my book bag. "Coach kept quizzing me about the new swimmers. Have I missed much?" I whispered to Mary, who was dressed in green from head to toe. Where did she ever find pickle-colored tights?

Mary shook her head. "We've just been goofing around with Mr. C. Now we're going over everyone's story ideas and weeding out the bad ones."

I raised my hand as soon as Sam finished taping blank sheets of newsprint across the chalkboard. "What's the deal with all the paper?"

Mr. Chicelli came forward to sit on the corner of his desk. "Sam thought we might put the stories into categories like sports, editorials, news, and general interest. You all may decide to use some and save others for upcoming issues."

Sam bowed toward me. "If that meets with your approval, oh bossy assistant, let's get the show on the road. Who's going first?"

I thought what a creep he was. "How about science fair plans?"

"Whoa," said Sam, writing my suggestion as he spoke. "Let's hope someone can make this sound interesting. Science fairs are snorers, same thing, year after year. People, give me something fun."

"How about a dance schedule?" asked Becky.

"Now that's an idea," said Sam. "More, more."

"Maybe we could cover activities for the Fall Festival," said Mary, in a soft voice.

"Is that a day where people bob for apples and sell crafts?" asked Sam, pretending to stifle a yawn.

I blinked. *Who does this guy think he is?* "It's way more than that. It's the biggest fund-raiser of the year."

Mr. Chicelli nodded. "Last year's proceeds bought new computers for the library."

"Got it," said Sam, putting the festival at the top of one list. "Don't mess with money, I mean tradition."

Brad cleared his throat, and said, "Another big tradition is the Turkey Bowl, the major soccer tournament in November."

"Cool," said Sam, putting that at the top of another sheet.

I said, "I thought we would be covering some real issues in the newspaper."

"Like what?" asked Mr. Chicelli.

"Well, maybe taking a stand against bullying or school vandalism or investigating things like who's killing all the fish."

"Fish?" asked one of the boys.

"A lot of fish have died out on the river," I said. "A whole bunch of them washed up on shore at my uncle's house."

"Hm, whereabouts is your uncle's place?" asked Mr. Chicelli.

"Just south of Walker's Bridge."

"Did someone shoot them?" asked Jamie Myers, a girl from my swim team. "Sometimes a bunch of good ol' boys start playing with BB guns and blast away. It's kind of gross, but it happens."

I shuddered, then shook my head. "There were hundreds of fish. Could they kill that many goofing around?"

Mr. Chicelli shook his head. "Not likely, if there were as many dead fish as you say. Odd we haven't heard about it. I suppose it could have just been some freak of nature."

"Yeah," agreed Sam, "like red tide—stinky and burns your eyes, but nothing to get our shorts in a knot over."

"Maybe not for you," I said, not wanting to give up, "but they said it's happened before. My relatives called the county and when someone finally came out he acted like it was my uncle's fault. Like he'd polluted the river with his apple orchard. I want to find out what really happened."

"Whoever's responsible, we should write about it," said Mary. "All those poor fish."

"Yeah, it's too bad, but they're *fish*," said Sam, staring out the window for a moment. "And maybe her uncle dumped some gas from his apple picker in the water and there they went, bellies up."

Mr. Chicelli cleared his throat. "Sam, you may be right. Still, this could be an interesting story. Why not let Emily do some research about fish and we'll consider it then."

"That sounds okay to me." Sam shrugged and wrote, "fish, dead" under the news category. "But it may get shoved to the bottom of the list. Kids I know would rather hear about swim meet scores or getting better food in the cafeteria than worry about a bunch of moldy fish. Shoot, I just had another great idea. How about an advice column? Or sports tips? Like how to improve your forehand? Sounds good, huh?"

As everyone in the room began nodding their heads, I thought of something better. "A column, written by Sam

Wheeler, and its title could only be, *Yes, I Am the Guy with All the Answers.*" Oops, did I say that out loud?

~

To put Sam out of my mind, after school I asked mom to take me to Aunt Sylvie's. It was the perfect day to go, as Dad was out of town for work. That also meant we'd be picking up pizza for dinner on the way home.

On the way out there, Mom asked, "What's in the little blue box?"

"Oh, something I borrowed from coach. One of my science teachers suggested it."

"Extra credit?"

"Not exactly," I said, as we pulled in behind my aunt and uncle's house. "Just me, gathering information. Y'know, girl reporter and all that." I bounded in the house, gave out hugs, and waited until Mom got inside with Ben. "Uncle Joe, remember how the county guy didn't test the water?"

"Sure do."

"Well, that's okay because you can do it yourself with this pool test kit I borrowed from Coach Anders."

"Honey, this is a river," said Aunt Sylvie.

Uncle Joe nodded. "Yes, but water's water. What are we testing for?"

"pH... you know, acidity and alkalinity. Plus, this kit has a little floating pool thermometer."

"All right, Missy, so we can check temperature, too. Show me how it's done."

Mom said, "Emily, how do you know about this?"

I shrugged. "Coach has some of us test the pool water when we get there early for practices. I talked to Ms. Smith some more in study hall about fish dying, and she said testing the river water would get us started on fact-finding about it. We're supposed to get water quality test kits this year for all the science classes, but they haven't come in yet. So, we'll start with this. It's sort of a twofer."

"Twofer?" asked Aunt Sylvie.

"Maybe I can find out something for you about what killed the fish, and at the same time, get a jump on my science project. Y'know, two for the price of one?"

"Well, you are not only a beautiful young lady," said Aunt Sylvie, "you are a smart one, too." She reached into a cupboard and came out with a cardboard box. "You might need something to put water in, so take some of my little canning jars. The jam size should be perfect."

I gave her a hug, and Uncle Joe and I walked down to the dock. I told him how to use the test strips. "pH measures acidity in a solution, like in our case, the river water. If pH is lower, the paper turns pink, and it means we have an acid."

"What if it's higher?"

"Then the paper turns blue and it means it's a base. You probably know this, but soap is a base but vinegar is an acid. Normal or neutral pH is 7. pH too far out of the middle can hurt or even kill the things that live in that water. Fish or turtles and other sea creatures like 6.5-8.0." Tonight, the pH paper turned purple, and the river tested 7.2.

I went on, trying to explain what the science teacher had told me. "Measuring acidity and alkalinity is important to figure out a stream or river's ability to fix itself. Like is it able to neutralize acidic pollution from rainfall or wastewater? We're measuring the water's ability to resist changes in pH. Sound smart, don't I?"

"Very much so."

"It was all Ms. Smith, but it actually makes sense, even to me. Uncle Joe, you need to note if it's real high or real low. I can leave some pH testing paper. If there's a big change, something's going on."

The water temperature that night was 74 degrees. We didn't know what normal was, but this would be our starting point. When we finished, I held out the little blue box. "Here you go, sir. You can keep all these results on the note cards I tucked inside the box."

Uncle Joe shook his head. "I'll just put them on a spreadsheet on my computer."

I grinned. "Right, Mr. Techie."

He handed the test kit back to me. "I'll head to the hardware store tomorrow. They've got a pool section, so I'll get a brand new one. You keep this."

I nodded. My uncle, a *nice* guy with all the answers.

CHAPTER 8

NOBODY'S FAULT

As soon as I got home from school on Wednesday, I made some notes that answered the question Sam had asked about how my aunt and uncle picked their apples. Before we left their house Monday night, Aunt Sylvie told me they harvested by hand, not with "a noisy, smelly, gasoline picking machine." She also said they hired a few neighbor kids to help, so while they might pitch some of the bruised apples into the river, they couldn't be polluting it or killing fish with six or seven rotten apples.

I did kind of wonder about the golf course. That county guy had said that "aquatic creatures" can be killed by weed killer and fertilizer, and those things are what greenskeepers typically use. I'd heard the course had a neat design with some greens that jutted out into the water. Since Leanne wouldn't help me, I wasn't sure who to talk to at the country club, so I started with the first person who answered the phone. A fancy-sounding lady quizzed me a few minutes but finally transferred me to the assistant golf pro whose name was John Wiley. I introduced myself and then said, "Sir, I'm doing some research for our school paper and possibly my science project. Do you have time to answer a few questions about golf course management?"

Mr. Wiley said, "Well, I'm pretty new here and still learning the ropes, but I guess I can give it a shot."

"Terrific. First, who decides when to cut the grass? And what types of fertilizer or weed killer do you use?"

He cleared his throat. "I thought you wanted to ask management questions. These sound like greenskeeper operations issues to me."

Rats, this had started off so well. What *are* greenskeeping operations? They don't teach you stuff like this in seventh grade. I plowed on. "Oh, um, who should I talk to, then?"

"Maybe the head pro, Mickey Smith. Let me see if he's available." Instantly, I was on hold again. Several minutes passed. I stretched the long, snaky phone cord so I could grab a snack from the pantry. I had just unwrapped a cookie when a new voice boomed through the receiver.

"Mickey Smith here. Is this Jensen's Pesticides?"

"No, sir. This is Emily Sanders. I'm on the school paper at Farleigh Middle and we wanted to know what sort of weed killer you use there at the course. And maybe what type of fertilizer, too."

"Did you say you're a middle schooler? Shouldn't you be asking me stuff like how far a golf ball travels or do we sell pink golf socks?"

I shook my head. Everyone was a comedian. "Normally that might be the type of question I would ask. But we're investigating a serious matter and are hoping you can help us get to the bottom of why so many fish in the Higdon River have died. They died not far from the golf course, part of which sits on the edge of the river. Did you mention a pesticide company when you answered the phone?"

"Nice try, young lady. Yes, I thought you were the rep from Jensen's. We use some of their granulated fertilizers where we can. We don't use big spray rigs. We've cut our mowing areas down and have silt fences to trap gunk. Also, we've put riprap wherever the course meets the river."

"Riprap is like they have up at the lake, right? A bunch of rocks kind of holding the bank up?"

"Correct. It helps with runoff. We also use recycled water for sprinkling and timers so we don't overwater. We've got a filtering system that acts like a sewer under the fairways and directs water to holding tanks like cisterns. Do you know what those are?"

"I do," I said. "You see 'em on historical buildings or at the beach. Kind of like water tanks that catch rainwater."

"Yes, in a manner of speaking. So, Miss Sanders, while I'm sorry about the fish, I don't believe our little golf course is your killer."

"Yes, sir, it sounds like you're off the hook. Sorry, bad pun."

He laughed. "No, it's actually quite funny. You're doing a good job. Feel free to stop out here anytime if you want to do any further investigating. Stinky fish could really ruin our golfers' day."

A click came through the receiver and I sat listening to the dial tone for a few minutes, pretending it was music. Now what? No apple-picking problems, and apparently no fish had died from crummy golf course operations. However, maybe I was crazy to trust those two golf guys. Maybe I should consider doing a little water test out there or take a walk around the greenskeeper's shed. Hmm, definitely something to think about.

Just in case this whole thing turned into a story written by yours truly, I put the apple orchard and golf course info into a notebook labeled, "NP (newspaper)." Having a notebook made me feel like a real reporter, but at this point all I had were some random notes. Maybe I was nuts to think I could get to the bottom of this. I munched the cookie.

Mom came in from a walk with Ben. "Hi, did I hear sighing?"

I reached down to help Ben off with his jacket. "I'm striking out trying to find fish killers. Any ideas?"

Mom said, "Hmm, Cousin Jerry might have some."

"Is Jerry the one who works at that sawmill? Are they big polluters?"

Mom looked quizzical. "I don't know. Sawmills are real messy but that wasn't what I meant."

I held up my hand. "Wait, I know. You meant he's out there along the river and might *see* things. He can be the family spy!"

Mom laughed. "Something like that. His number is in my cell phone."

I rummaged through her bag, found the phone and her list of names, and dialed. I was beginning to feel like a real reporter checking out sources. Unfortunately, no one answered, so I left a message and sighed again. There were no more excuses to avoid the math homework peeking out of my book bag. I trudged to my room.

Later, when I had finally finished every speck of homework, had taken a shower and was shoving my feet into bunny slippers, Mom tapped on the bathroom door. "Em, Cousin Jerry called while you were in the shower."

I opened the door. "Is it too late to call him back?"

"I think so. He said it's hard to catch him on the phone, but if you want to come out to the sawmill he can show you around and talk out there. Problem is, for the next couple of days, I'm helping out at Ben's preschool in the afternoons."

I shrugged. "No biggie. I'll ride my bike out there. What is it, a couple miles?"

"Oh, at least, but it's supposed to be pretty the rest of the week. If you ride out there, I can swing by and pick you up so you can ride home with us."

"Great. I'm going to try one thing. Maybe Leanne would go with me. Can't you just see her tromping around a sawmill?"

My mom laughed and headed for her bedroom. "Good luck with that."

She was right, but I sprinted to my room and called Leanne anyway. When I got hold of her, I presented the bike trip like it was an adventure she couldn't pass up.

"You are asking me to ride my bike, what, like fifty miles? After a whole day at school?"

"Come on, it's five miles, maybe, roundtrip. Ten tops. I'll buy you a snack at Milton's Grocery."

"That's a gas station, hardly a grocery store."

"They have Moon Pies."

"True, but the only reason I'd consider going is I'm getting fat. I need the exercise."

I thought about that for a minute. Leanne was like a stick figure, so tall she'd never get fat. There was just too much of her to ever get fluffed up. "You are crazy. Fat should not be a word you ever utter."

Leanne cleared her throat. "Okay, thanks. I probably needed to hear that. Truth is, I've had to babysit like every day lately, and it's driving me crazy. But you are too. Do you realize the only subject you ever talk to me about is fish? It seems like it's taking over your entire life."

"Yeah, it is. I'm focusing on it now, because once swim season starts, I'll have no time. So, it's fish now or never."

"Well, tempting as you've made it, I'm a 'no' to the sawmill run. I'd say let me know what you find out, but honestly, I think it's a big waste of your time. Oops, I've got another call. Bye."

And Leanne was gone, again. Maybe in more than one way.

~

The next afternoon, as sweat drizzled down my neck, I was kind of glad Leanne hadn't come with me. She'd have been whining the whole time, because it had turned out to be one of those hot Indian summer days. Normally, the fall air felt crisp and cool, but today the late sun beat down like a heat lamp and there was not one whisper of wind. Thankfully, I was almost at the sawmill, so I concentrated on pedaling and soon I bumped across the gravel parking lot, waving to my second cousin, Jerry. He looked like the basketball star he had once been, tall and relaxed. He was dressed in jeans, leather work boots, and a baseball-style jacket with a tree logo on it. His hair was the same chocolate-bar color as Mom's with an identical reddish tinge. I guessed the red concentrated in one place with me. He took his thick, ribbed gloves off and gave me a hug.

"Glad to see you, young lady," Jerry said, pointing toward the side of a long one-story wooden building where I could park my bike. "So, you want to learn the sawmilling business, do you?"

I pushed my bike just past the door marked "Office" and leaned it against the wall. "Well, I guess I do. What I wondered is if what you do here could pollute the Higdon River."

"Pollute?" asked Jerry, taking off his baseball cap and scratching his head, just like Uncle Joe. Grandma would say they were cut from the same cloth. "Hmm, I don't see how we'd actually pollute the river. The only time our logs touch the water is while they're being moved down here from the mountains. Mostly they come on eighteen-wheel trucks but sometimes they have to get floated down the river. In the early spring, the river doesn't ice over, but the mountain roads freeze and are so slick the trucks can't get around without sliding off the edge, so they float the logs then. Let me show you what we do."

He gave me a neon yellow hard hat and earplugs, which was nice since the saws were screeching in every direction. Jerry pointed toward a sign that said, "Flammable - Gasoline in Use," and then at two saws slicing through some skinny planks. He shouted, "Special order, flooring." He handed me some goggles, and all I could think about as I slid them on was what Leanne would have said if she'd come with me. I felt like some kind of space alien, but nobody even glanced at me. The giant wood chipper looked like a hungry dinosaur noisily chomping bark and other limbs as fast as the two guys operating it could shove in more wood. Jerry motioned me to a spot out of the way of its spewing bark particles. "In the old days, if you were asking about *air pollution* I might have had to let you speak to our attorney and the project manager. We do burn a bit of wood here and there, but nowadays most every piece of a log gets used for something."

We walked over to a structure that looked like a metal train car with conveyor belts running through it. Workers shut the doors on either end, and I could feel heat oozing from the vents spaced around the corners of the structure. Jerry tipped his head and said, "That's our newest gadget, a dryer."

"What's it for?"

"It's for removing moisture from the wood. Kiln drying is the fancy term and it speeds up everything, so my boss makes money quicker and that's good for me, you know?"

I pointed toward a huge shovel scooping sawdust into what looked like a giant bread pan. Water and some gunky stuff squirted onto the sawdust, and then men with big paddles stirred the mixture as it went down a conveyor and disappeared into a building. "Guess you don't burn up the sawdust either?"

He grinned. "Now you're catching on. That's the start of making particle board."

"What's that used for?" I asked.

"Oh, gosh, tons of things like kitchen cabinets or the frame of your living room sofa. We use a non-formaldehyde resin to hold it together."

"Is there any dangerous runoff from making particle board? Like stray wood chips? Resin? Something like that?"

"Good question. While we do wash the wood chips before using them, the water is filtered before going into the river. And so, no runoff from us."

I shook my head. "Unless you accidentally dump a bunch of gasoline into the river, I don't see where you could be killing any fish."

Jerry scuffed the dirt with his workboot. "Okay, I see where you're going with this. I've heard rumors of a bunch of fish showing up dead now and then. Wish I could help you."

"Yup, me too, and so does Aunt Sylvie."

Jerry looked puzzled. "This happened out by their place?"

"At least twice, maybe more." We walked toward the entrance to the property. I handed Jerry the hardhat, earplugs and goggles. "Mom should be here soon, so I'll just wait by the gate. Thanks for showing me around."

"Anytime," Jerry said, taking the goggles. Then he tapped me on the arm. "Have you checked any of the factories upriver?"

I shook my head. "No, not yet. The guy from the county told Uncle Joe that it couldn't have been any of them because they have regulations to abide by or something like that."

He nodded. "Well, he could be right or he could just be lazy. Some of those county boys don't want to fill out any more reports than they have to. I'm glad it's not us, but I wish I could have been more help. If I hear of anything out this way, I'll let you know."

Thinking, *Another dead end*, I summoned up a smile. "Thanks, Jerry. It was kind of neat out here. Loud, but neat. If it's okay, on my way out I'm gonna grab water samples for my science project." I went down to the river's edge near where the logs floated up. How did something that huge float? I pulled two jars from my bag, scooped some river water, checked and noted the water temp, and headed over to get my bike. Just as I stuffed the samples away, Mom drove up. She opened the back of the car, and I shoved my bike and backpack in next to a couple of bags of groceries. I plopped into the front seat, and said, "Another theory bites the dust. And I do mean dust." I brushed off the sleeves of my jacket, and pointed to a billow of sawdust as the giant scooper grabbed another load.

"Oh, Emily, I'm sorry. It looks like a messy place."

I looked around. "It's majorly messy. I got some water samples, and I'll test them at home. But, it doesn't look like they do anything here that would kill a fish, unless a log rolled over on one. I may just have to tell Aunt Sylvie I can't help them. The fish are on their own."

CHAPTER 9
FOOTBALL FOR FISH

Monday, I hurried and caught Sam after Phys Ed. I poked around in my backpack as we walked down the hall. "Why is it everything I need always disappears in here? I wanted to ask you about my story but I don't see it. Maybe it's in—"

Sam grabbed my arm but couldn't stop me from running headfirst into Cynthia Craver. "Cynthia, I didn't see you!"

"Of course not, silly, you've always got your head buried in some notebook," Cynthia said. "You don't even know you're walking with the cutest guy in two counties."

Sam gave us a profile pose like a movie star, and said, "Trust me, Emily knows what's here, but she values me more for my boss-like qualities."

"That must be it," said Cynthia, scooping her arm through his. "Everybody knows Emily's too wrapped up in your silly school paper to have time for boys. Right, Em?"

I stood in the hall, once again stumped for the perfect reply. The best I could manage was, "Right, just me and a pencil."

"That works for me," said Sam, "'cuz you're making my job easier."

"Well, isn't that just peachy," said Cynthia, tugging Sam's arm. "Now, are you gonna let me buy you lunch before I pass out from starvation?"

"I'm ready," said Sam, holding his stomach. "Em, we'll talk at the meeting tomorrow. See ya."

I stood staring after them until someone nudged me from behind.

"Oh, hi, Leanne."

Leanne nodded toward the cooing couple. "Just think, we'll have boyfriends too some day."

I didn't say anything as we walked down the hall toward the cafeteria. Stuff was just happening so fast in seventh grade. Everywhere I turned there were changes, from my body to my classes. I could barely keep up with the homework load and the newspaper, plus swim practice would be starting soon. And now I was supposed to think about boys? I gazed around the cafeteria not seeing one prime candidate. "Boyfriends? No time soon, at least for me. So, what did you bring for lunch?"

Leanne sniffed. "Gosh, Em, isn't your nose twitching in anticipation? It's pizza day—and Cynthia's buying!"

I sighed and said, "This is just perfect. I've got a peanut butter sandwich and carrot sticks and you get free pizza."

"Sorry," said Leanne, as she took off for the food line. "Want me to get you some milk? I'm sure Cyn wouldn't mind."

I could see Sam and Cynthia motioning for Leanne to join them. "You go on, I'm not very thirsty. See you later." I trudged out of the cafeteria feeling like a stranger in my own school. Enter Cynthia, exit Emily. After managing to make it through the front door, I went outside and plopped down on the steps and buried my face on my knees.

A few minutes later a soft voice said, "Emily, are you all right?"

I looked up to see Mary Carnell's worried face peering at me. "Hi, Mary. I'm okay, it's just I don't like it when stuff in my life changes. I'll get over it."

Mary hesitated and then sat down on the step below me. She arranged her denim skirt so it covered her eyelet petticoat and ankle-high leather boots. A sky-colored sweater trimmed in more eyelet was tucked into the skirt. A purple and navy suede belt cinched her waist.

For a moment, I stared at Mary, thinking no one wore their skirts that long, but on her the dramatic seemed normal. "Where do you get your clothes?"

Mary grinned, and said, "At a store, like everyone else! Except it's my grandma's shop in New York City, so I guess I sometimes wear stuff that nobody else would." She shrugged and began to eat some yogurt. She took small dainty bites, then carefully licked the spoon. "I come out here a lot to eat my lunch."

I glanced around at the worn granite steps. "Why?"

"Well, sometimes I pick up trash. In the olden days, my parents would have been hippies. Ever since I was a little kid, they've dragged me along on volunteer cleanup crews for things like 'Keep America Beautiful', 'Save the Planet', and all that."

I nodded. "Yeah, my mom's a big garden clubber and does that stuff, too. I guess here you don't find too many gross things, but along the highway—ugh!"

"For sure," Mary agreed. "Hmm, what else do I do out here at lunch? I like to look at stuff, like the flowering trees along the sidewalk in the spring or the flag waving in the wind. Probably sounds stupid."

"Nope, no more stupid than trying to stay friends with someone who doesn't want you anymore."

"I'm sure that hurts."

"It really does, a whole bunch," I said, pulling my sandwich and carrots from my lunch bag. "Let's talk about something else. So, you eat and look around?"

"Well, I will for a few more months." Mary shivered. "Then I have to move inside or sit out here in the snow!"

We laughed and ate in silence. Then Mary spoke. "Are you still checking on the dead fish?"

I nodded. "It's kind of weird. I looked up a bunch of stuff, and apparently, fish die for a lot of different reasons."

"Really?"

"Yeah, but, so far, only three would be remotely possible here. One of them is pollution, from toxic waste dumped into the water. So, I started checking businesses that might be responsible. Ms. Smith suggested getting water samples and testing them."

"Is that hard to do?"

I shook my head. "Right now, I'm just using a pool test kit."

Mary looked like she was thinking about something. "We have a pool. I know exactly what you mean. Good idea. I never thought about it working with a river."

"Well, my uncle's testing water at his place every day." I shrugged. "So far, there hasn't been much to report. I got a water sample out at the sawmill the other day and tested it. Basically, it was normal pH, at the higher end of normal, just a little high in alkalinity. Nothing off the charts." I sighed. "The main places I've checked with so far don't seem to be guilty of anything that would kill that many fish, even once."

"So, at this point, probably not pollution. What else harms fishies?"

"Well, lack of oxygen can be bad and so can hot/cold temperature fluctuations. My uncle and I are also testing temperatures, and I think I'll be checking on oxygen when the school test kits come in. When I read this stuff, it kind of freaks me out. I'm not that great in science."

Mary shrugged. "Hey, you don't have to be great in science. You just have to make enough sense to get people who *are* great in science to listen to you."

"True, but I don't want to keep running to the teacher like a little baby. The thing is, I can't figure what to do next. Someone suggested checking out the factories. But there are so many of them. Where do I start?"

Mary squinted up toward the sky as if she were thinking hard. "Emily, try something with me. When I paint, first I see whatever I'm painting in my mind. Can you picture the river?"

I closed my eyes, thinking we definitely looked stupid, but I would go with it for a minute. "Okay, I see it."

"Great. Now, you see farms, parks, bridges, houses, and lots of factories. Right?"

I shook my head. "I see all that along the river but not that many factories."

Mary poked me with her boot. "Correct. I think we're seeing the same thing."

"We might be." I grabbed my NP notebook and said, "Draw." She sketched as I watched over her shoulder. "I'm such a goof. You've just drawn Watson Tables and Cayenne Textiles. Those two sit right on the edge of the river. The towel plant on the Higden River in Danville is forty miles away. I'm thinking that wouldn't count."

"Maybe, maybe not," said Mary, tapping her drawing. "Where do I put the dead fish?"

I pointed to a spot below Walker's Bridge, where Aunt Sylvie's house should be on this drawing which was quickly turning into a map. "Right there."

Mary quickly sketched in some fish, then studied the drawing. "I think you can cross off the place in Danville. So, are you just going to barge into two big ol' factories here?"

I giggled. "That would be hilarious, but probably not very smart. I guess I need to do more research, like how they make stuff."

"Do you need help?"

My mouth dropped open. "You'd do that?"

"Why not?" asked Mary, brushing a speck of dust off her boots.

"I'm just surprised. Everyone I know thinks this is just a big waste of time." I flipped through my notebook, and said, "I'll check how Watson makes tables, and the other place tube tops, but could you make some phone calls?"

"Sure, I can handle that," answered Mary.

"That would be great. I need to find out any other places besides Aunt Sylvie's where fish have died on the Higdon. I looked up the numbers of some marinas and that Country Corner grocery store."

"That's good. Oh, there's the fish camp and a farm supply store."

"Good ideas. Otherwise, it's just pretty woodsy out there."

"True. So, I'll start calling right after school," Mary said, putting the paper in her book bag. "Um, two things. That sweater looks good with your hair."

I glanced down at my sleeves. Once I get dressed, I honestly never think about how I look. "Thanks, it was the first clean thing I could find."

Mary smiled. "It would also look good under a vest or with a scarf."

I was stunned. I never would have thought of putting something on top of a top. "Okay, I'll remember that."

"If you ever want someone to go shopping with you, I'd go."

Honestly, I'd much rather have a tooth pulled than go shopping, but apparently this was an important skill. It sure was to my f. f. (former friend) Leanne. "Again, okay. That might be helpful."

Mary nodded. "Just let me know. The second thing is, do you ever go to the Elgin High football games?"

"Sure, I go to all the home games. Why?"

"Well, my cousin is the starting quarterback this year," answered Mary, "and I have no idea what he does. Could you go to a game with me and explain it?"

"Oh, Leanne and I always go to the games together..." I stopped abruptly. Who knew if we'd go together now? Things were so different. I sat thinking for a minute and then made a decision. "I love football. Count me in." Suddenly, football for fish seemed like a fair trade.

CHAPTER 10
LEARN MORE,
KNOW LESS

After school that day, I sprinted off the bus and cut across three backyards and a bunch of driveways, trying to get home before Ben got up from his nap. As I burst in the front door, I remembered. Mom was helping at his pre-school in the afternoons, so they weren't even home yet. Rats! I am a member of a loving, yet most annoyingly strict, family when it comes to computers. We have one machine in our house, and I am not allowed to even turn it on or press a key, let alone go online, unless a parent is home. I needed to do some quick searches about those two factories. Come on, Mom!

No choice but to fix a snack. Peanut butter, crackers, and a knife were all I needed to make after-school food heaven. I washed it down with some of Aunt Sylvie's cider and paced by the front door until I finally heard Mom's car in the driveway. I peeked out the dining room window and saw my worst, time-consuming nightmare. Bags and bags of groceries! I flung open the door and dashed to the car. "Hi, want some help?"

Mom stood by the back car door staring at me with those probing parent eyes. "I'd love it. What will *this* cost me?"

"Cost?" I asked, hoping for an innocent tone.

"Hmmm." Mom grabbed a few bags and Ben's little hand, and headed for the house. "Can you get the rest? When we've put everything away, you can come clean and tell me what I'm going to owe you for this."

I snagged what seemed like a hundred bags and staggered to the house, plopping everything on the kitchen counter. I gave Ben a couple of my amazing peanut butter crackers to keep him occupied. "I need to go online to do some research."

"A term paper already?"

"No, fish stuff for the school paper."

Mom gave me one of those "don't push me" looks. "As important as this is to our family, are you putting dead fish ahead of your homework?"

I shook my head. "No, I'm getting everything done. Tonight all I have is vocabulary words."

71

"All right. Use the computer for one hour, then come see me and we'll discuss if you need more time. And no e-mail until after we talk. Deal?"

I grabbed my notebook and pencil. "Deal, Mom. Have I mentioned that no other kid at my school has as many restrictions as I do?"

"Thankfully, you've failed to mention that today. Your minutes are ticking, Missy!"

I took the stairs two at a time and fired up the computer in the spare bedroom/office. I did a search for Watson Tables, and five pages of information postings appeared. In 1899 two Watson brothers made a conference table for a local attorney. He liked the first table, ordered three more, and the Watsons had a new business. Now, the company had three locations in two states and employed over 400 people. Other than needing water for steam to bend wood to form chair backs, I wondered if this company needed to be on a river to make sofas or headboards. I wrote the company phone number in my notebook and glanced at the computer screen to check the time. Other kids can spend hours playing solitaire or chatting with their friends on their computers. Me? Tick, tock, tick, tock. I grabbed the phone and dialed, wondering what department to ask for. A breath-less sounding woman answered, "Watson Tables. How may I direct your call?"

When I hesitated a split second the voice directed, "Hold, please." I listened to some jazz, and in a few seconds, she was back. I jumped in. "My name is Emily and I'm a student doing a report. Is there someone I could talk to about the history of the company?"

"Hmm," the lady said, "not really. Let me—oops, gotta put you on hold again, honey." And she was gone, returning in just a few seconds. "Sorry, it's like this every day the closer it gets to five o'clock. Now, you probably need our director of advertising and communications, but he's at pre-market in High Point. I'm Nell, and I've been here for a jillion years so maybe I could help. Talk fast."

"I'm doing a story on pollution and I wondered if Watson Tables has ever been in any trouble for polluting say, the river."

"Wow, you don't pull any punches. Are you a college student?"

"Nope, middle school."

"Again, wow. Okay, you'd really have to speak with one of the engineers, but from what I understand, the company has never had any citations for *water* pollution, but years ago, the air quality around this plant really stunk. So, they brought in a bunch of scientists who revamped every smokestack, burner and assembly line to be—oh, what is that fancy phrase, um, 'in compliance', that's it. We are a clean plant now."

I sighed. "That's great. However, my report is about the water in the Higdon."

"Sorry, honey. Wish I could be more help."

"It's okay, but I do have one other question. Does the factory need water to make furniture?"

"Water? Do you mean like for washing hands, mixing stains or lacquer? That kind of water?"

"No, um, I guess I mean, why was a furniture factory built on a river?"

"Oh, the light bulb in my brain has just blinked on," Nell answered. "Our founding fathers, the Watsons, were given this land by their granddaddy and they sawmilled on this very spot for years. Then one of 'em got the bright idea to make something besides lumber from the logs they brought down the river. First they made tables, then chairs, and a factory just grew right around where the sawmill had been. So, we don't *have* to be on the river now, but here we are. And you should see all we do."

"I *did* see some things on the website. It's cool stuff, but it doesn't look like y'all dump toxic waste into the river."

"You got it, sugar, but if you find anyone who does, let me know. They should be hog-tied."

I giggled. "It's a deal, Nell. Thank you so much."

"No problem. Gotta go, girl. It's five o'clock and I may be a granny, but I've got a date."

Just think, if I were a normal girl, I might have a date, too. But, no, I have it in my head that I'm some kind investigative reporter who can't get any results.

Plunging on, next I did a search for Cayenne Textiles and found it was started in the early 1900s by a group of investors. It had several different names over the years and in the beginning just made fabric like muslin. Today, they made clothes, mostly sweatsuits, athletic jerseys, or pajamas. Crazy colors were their claim to fame.

It was too late to call their offices, but I thought about what else I'd like to know. I searched for history of fabrics and textiles in America and quickly scanned the story. I kept seeing the words *water* and *rivers*. I learned that "Waterwheel-powered textile machines and fabric-making factories use tons of water" and "Dyes, discharge, and temperatures can affect river systems often with disastrous results."

Ding, ding, ding!!! A factory like Cayenne was located on a river because it needed water! And fish *live* in that water. Or in our case, die. Talk about disastrous results. I hoped there was ink in our printer.

CHAPTER 11

BACK IT UP

Tuesday, when the bell rang dismissing my last class, I hung around a few moments until most of the kids had left. I scooped up my papers and book bag and went to the front of the room to speak to my science teacher, Ms. Allen. She wasn't the department chair like my 6th grade teacher, Ms. Smith was, but I was hoping she would help me. "Ms. Allen, do you know much about the textile industry?"

"Textiles?"

I nodded. "Yes, ma'am. You know, shirts, towels, socks, stuff like that."

"Well, I know we make a lot of those things around here, but what exactly are you trying to find out?"

"Um, I was wondering if it's a dangerous industry."

Ms. Allen sat back in her chair. "Dangerous? To the workers?"

"Oh, sure, to the workers, and maybe to other things like the environment."

"Are you doing some creative writing thing for English? These are odd questions, unless you might have decided on pollution for your science project."

I grinned, thinking science teachers all talk the same language sometimes. "Well, I *might* tackle pollution for my project and would definitely talk to you, but actually, this is for the school paper."

Ms. Allen rubbed her hands together as if she held a delicate secret between them. "I love it. You're doing an investigative report."

I laughed. "I wish. So far, all I have are a bunch of dead ends to write about."

"Well, that's how many scientific discoveries have been made. And I bet many news breaks happen because a reporter doesn't give up on a story."

I tapped my pencil. "That's how it is for me. I mean the not giving up part. It's just the dead ends make you wonder if you really have a story."

"Well, all those scientists we're studying? People laughed at many of them at first." Ms. Allen glanced at the clock on the wall. "I'm so sorry, but I've got to leave for a dentist's appointment. As far as the textile industry around here and pollution, I don't have any direct knowledge. Sorry I can't be more help. However, I'd say probably *water* pollution would be the most likely problem they might have to watch out for."

I felt like squirming in my chair like a kid waiting to blow out the candles on her birthday cake. Instead, I said, "Hmm, water pollution makes sense. Listen, don't worry about having to leave. I've got to get to a newspaper meeting. Thanks so much." I turned to leave.

"Wait, you're the one!"

"Ma'am?"

"We're going to do a unit on water quality next semester. The first shipment of water quality test kits just arrived, and Ms. Smith sent one down to me marked 'E. S., student, 7th grade'. I didn't understand her 'code', but it's clear to me now she meant Emily Sanders!" She spun around in her desk chair, searching through a gigantic tote bag. Finally, she pulled out a little red box and waved it in the air. "Here you go."

I nodded. "She said these were delayed in shipment. Um, are there directions inside?"

"Let's see." Ms. Allen slit the seal and opened the lid. "Hm, it looks a lot like the pool test kits, doesn't it?" She scanned through the little pamphlet, and nodded. "You should be fine. There's a little thermometer in here, and the only additional thing in this kit is a test for dissolved oxygen. Are you familiar with that?"

"Ms. Smith told me about it, and I've also done some research."

Ms. Allen grabbed her tote bag, pointed to the clock, and said, "I'm so sorry, but I have to head out. It sounds like you have a grasp of what to do, but please read the directions tonight and we'll talk again in class tomorrow. How's that for a plan?"

"Sounds great, see you then," I said, grabbing the kit. "Good luck at the dentist." I sprinted to Mr. Chicelli's room as quickly as I could without looking dorky and arrived right as Sam said, "Any more story ideas?"

I threw up my hand. "Remember the dead fish issue?"

"Issue?" asked Sam. "How big an issue can it be? They're either dead or not."

As a couple kids laughed, I shook my head. "Very funny. Mr. C. told me I could do some research and I have."

Mr. Chicelli said, "What are your findings, Emily?"

"Well, there has been red tide in Virginia, but not in fresh water. I checked out some businesses on the river like a sawmill and the golf course. I have pages of details." I glanced up at Sam. "Don't worry, I won't read everything, but basically, they seem to run their places very responsibly. Do you want specifics?"

Sam shook his head. "Not me. Anyone else?"

Mary raised her hand. "Um, I've been helping Emily and we figured out that the area where the most fish have died is south of Walker's Bridge."

Mr. Chicelli cleared his throat. "Yes, she told us that before."

Mary nodded. "Right. But it's also south of two major factories, Watson Tables and Cayenne Textiles."

"Not the greatest sweatshirt factory in the world?" asked Betsey, pretending to hold a microphone, like a television announcer.

Someone else murmured, "Our fabrics are cool, our colors are hot."

"Maybe so," I answered, "but Cayenne might not be so hot if they're polluting the river. The stuff I've found out shows the furniture factory doesn't need water to make tables, but, and I quote, 'Fabric-making factories use tons of water. Dyes, discharge, and temperatures can affect river systems, often with disastrous results.'"

The kids in the room started whispering and Sam said, "Okay, you dug up some quotes. Is that supposed to be enough to make our school newspaper accuse some big shot factory about polluting the river?"

Mr. Chicelli said, "No accusations, Sam, but we may have an interesting story. Emily and Mary, however, *do* have to get more facts to backup this theory. We won't publish it until they do."

I slipped Mary a note that read "Fact-checking mission after school tomorrow?"

She read it, then grinned and nodded.

I put my hand to my ear and mouthed, "Call me."

"Personally," said Brad, "I'd hate to see us bad-mouthing Cayenne for something that could be a random freak of nature. My dad works there. I wish we'd just stick to school news."

"Point taken, big guy," said Sam. "I know some of those Cayenne people personally. They don't strike me as fish-killer types. So, let's let the fact-checkers see what they can dig up. Meanwhile, we'll write about things people care about, sports scores and edible food in the cafeteria, not what-ifs about moldy fish. Don't forget, there's always my advice column, *Ask Sam!*"

All I wanted to ask was when he was moving back to Greensboro.

CHAPTER 12

PUTTING AROUND

Wednesday, I met Mary at the corner of Old Newton Road and Highway 9 for our fact-finding mission. Okay, that sounds geeky, but it felt like we were undercover as we pedaled our bikes into River Landings Golf and Country Club. The guy at the guard gate probably wouldn't have let us in except Mary had suggested I bring a few putters and golf balls from our basement, so we actually looked like golfers. Well, maybe more like 'golfers-to-be', but still kind of like we belonged there. I've ridden a boy's bike for years, so it wasn't hard to strap the putters to the crossbar and throw a few balls in my backpack with some canning jars. I'd put stickers on the jars so we could mark them with the date and collection site. Mary had her cell phone, which had a camera too, so spying-wise, we were all set.

"Okay," I said, once we got past the guard gate, "where do we go now?"

Mary tilted her head toward the clubhouse.

I shook my head. "I don't think we're dressed for that place."

She said, "I know, just follow me." She pedaled toward the clubhouse, so I followed her down the drive and into the parking lot beside the fancy pillared building. We parked our bikes in the rack, and while she fiddled with her lock, I stood gazing toward the first hole of the course. It was impressive. You teed off toward a hole that was on an island in the river. You got to the green by crossing a little bridge only wide enough for a golf cart. This place was great.

Mary nudged me, so I stopped daydreaming about becoming a pro on the tour, grabbed a putter and some golf balls, and we took off. We passed the front of the two-story clubhouse, with floor to ceiling glass windows overlooking the river. The ground level held the pro shop where golf shirts, shorts, and pants glowed like wildflowers. Brand-name golf shoes and clubs stood ready for sale, and the Cayenne logo flashed in neon from the entrance. This place was huge, but finally we came to the putting green. It was sort of off by itself, teetering right on the edge of the water, and conveniently, was not occupied by any golfers at the moment.

"How did you know about this?" I asked.

Mary shrugged. "My grandma up in New York belongs to a club like this. She's a great golfer. I've gotten to play with her a few times. Every clubhouse has a putting green somewhere so players can warm up. Haven't you ever been with your dad?"

I shook my head. "My mom's the golfer in our family, but she quit playing when Ben was born. I don't remember if she played here or not." I looked around at the gorgeous flowers, heavy wrought iron light fixtures, and furniture scattered through the gardens. The driving range was beyond the putting green toward the entrance of the place, and the river stretched out as a rippling backdrop to the whole scene. "Um, what do we do now? Go get the samples?"

Mary shook her head. "If anyone is looking out the windows of the clubhouse, I think it should appear like we belong here. So far, so good. Let's take a few putts."

That made sense, so we grabbed our golf equipment, and soon, we were putting like we owned the joint. I was pretty good at lining up the shot, but kept hitting the ball too hard so it dribbled off the green every time. Mary was great at putting and made a lot of shots. We started making up scenarios like the ones golfers get into on TV. Then one of my shots bounced off the green and plopped into the river making an impressive splash. I got laughing so hard I thought I would fall down. Several people who appeared to be staff members came by and shushed us.

Mary said, "We better get off the radar screen up here while we can. We need to find some place to scoop up the samples. Keep your putter, one ball, and stick the jars in your pockets. We'll leave your bag with the bikes."

"Sounds good," I said, thinking Mary definitely had 'future spy' written all over her. We circled the clubhouse toward the parking lot. As we passed a little storage building where there were tubs of lawn care chemicals stacked up, Mary snapped a few photos. When we got to our bikes, I grabbed the jars and strapped my backpack onto my bike where the clubs had been, and we took off toward the golf course itself. I asked, "Do you know where we're going?"

Mary shook her head and pointed her putter. "I've got no idea, but it seems like we need to just keep heading toward the river. Some of these holes will have trees and bushes around them, so that'll give us some cover. Whatever you do, if anyone asks, just say we're looking for our grandfather."

I shrugged, not really understanding what she meant.

Mary went on. "We've got to act like we're members here, or they'll boot us out for sure. Let's pretend to be cousins. We're about the same height, weight, and except that you are beautiful, we even sort of look alike."

I couldn't believe what I was hearing. For the second time in the same week, someone had said I was beautiful. What was going on? Had a fairy godmother crept in my room recently? I was okay-looking, but beautiful? No way.

"Well, we do sort of look alike, but you're the cute, cheer-leader type, so I think that makes us even. So, we're looking for our grandfather? Cool, what's his name? Grandpa?"

"I think we might need a name. Gotta keep it simple, so just go with John Smith."

Just then, a man driving a golf cart shot by us, then stopped and turned in his seat. "Can I help you kids?"

Mary spoke up. "Not right now. We're looking for our grandpa. He's supposed to give us some putting tips."

The man nodded and got out of the cart. He must have assumed our grandpa was a member because he stuck out his hand and said, "Mickey Smith, head pro."

My 'cousin' stuck out her hand and said, "Mary Car-nell. Funny coincidence, our grandpa is John Smith."

The pro laughed and turned to me. I realized cousins don't need to have the same last name, so I just blurted out like always, "Emily Sanders." It dawned on me too late that this was the same guy I'd talked to on the phone. Probably mistake number one in spy school.

"Pleased to meet you girls. If I hear that Mr. Smith is on site, I'll send him your way." He shoved his mono-grammed visor up a bit, then scratched his head. "Have we met before, Emily?"

Great, I thought. He meets and talks to a jillion peo-ple everyday, but remembers a kid's name from a minute-long phone conversation? I decided to wing it. "No, sir, I don't think we've ever met."

He tipped his visor, and said, "Your name just sounded familiar. So, you two have fun out here and please stay on the cart paths unless you are putting." And he took off, the golf cart going at top speed.

As soon as he was out of sight around the next bunker, I grabbed Mary. "Eek, that was the guy I talked to on the phone. The one who insisted they do things safely out here."

Mary shrugged. "They probably do, so let's go get the samples and prove it."

We followed the path until we were almost to the river and one of the greens that jutted out into the water. I got the jars and trusty floating thermometer out of my pockets. We each scooped up some river water, then decided to retrieve some stray golf balls that had covered the bottom of the little cove, when another cart came whizzing out of nowhere. I had notated the water temp and stuffed everything back into my pockets, but there we stood, hands full of golf balls.

It was Mickey Smith again, this time with a grim look on his face. "Is it just coincidence that you are on our little course, or have you come to ask more pollution questions?"

"I guess it would be coincidence."

"Well, I need to ask you girls to leave. We do have two members named John Smith. One died last month, and the other is married to our banquet manager. Next time you come out, please make an appointment and someone will escort you around."

"Wait," I said, trying not to sound freaked out. "On the phone you said anytime I wanted to do more investigating, stop in."

He nodded. "True enough. But sneaking around and lying about things makes you appear more like trespassers than investigators."

Ouch, I thought. This whole reporting thing was complicated. "We're sorry."

Mary nodded. "Yes, sir. Where would you like us to put the golf balls we found?"

"Just drop them right there. Someone will be by for them later. You have ten minutes to get to the front gate or wherever you parked your bicycles. Any delay, I'll have no choice but to call the police. This is a private club." And he was off, golf cart wheels squealing as he headed toward the clubhouse.

Mary and I didn't speak while we dropped the balls as directed. We arranged them in a heart shape, grateful for not being arrested.

CHAPTER 13
CHILL IS IN THE AIR

It was the usual Friday lunch choice: fish stick surprise or the salad bar. I was trying to make up my mind when Leanne tapped me on the shoulder. "Come sit with me when you get through the line."

I nodded, thinking how long it had been since we'd eaten lunch together. I hummed happily, assembled my salad, grabbed two milks, and plopped down beside Leanne. "I can't believe you're sitting with me. Or that you're solo."

"I'm by myself because we need to talk," said Leanne in a low voice. "And if you don't watch out, you're going to be the one who's all alone."

Suddenly realizing this was no friendly lunch reunion, I asked, "What did I do?"

89

"You ran your mouth," said Leanne, folding her arms like a judge. "You should try keeping some of your opinions to yourself."

"Like which ones?"

"First, about the fish, of course, since now that's all you ever talk about," answered Leanne. "Second, who caused it. Sam said you were blabbing about it at the newspaper meeting. Fish die for lots of reasons, you said it yourself. It could be the golf course or some crazy boaters, you don't know. The Cayenne plant doesn't have anything to do with those stupid fish dying."

"How would you know?"

"The owner happens to be a personal friend," replied Leanne.

"So now you know some big conglomerate from New York?"

Leanne sighed one of her best stage sighs. "You are so pitiful. As of this past summer, Buford T. Craver has controlling interest in the Cayenne Corporation. Ring any bells? Cynthia's great-grandfather was one of the people who started the company back in the day, and now Mr. Craver has taken control of the whole operation."

"I remember you said her dad worked there. I didn't know he *owned* it."

Leanne shook her head. "It's more than that. He's trying to save it. You know a lot of companies around here have gone out of business?"

"Yeah, I know the towel factory closed in June and that little table plant by the hospital shut down in the past couple of weeks. Guess a bunch of our neighbors are out of work."

"Right. People who *have* jobs are happy they've still got them. And with Mr. Craver trying to turn things around he's pretty popular. He thinks Cynthia should major in design so she can work with him and help carry on the company."

"Of course," I said, stabbing around in my salad for stray croutons. "The fashion queen."

"Em," said Leanne, slapping the table, "why do you hate her so much?"

I bit my lip, then spoke. "I don't hate Cynthia. I just don't like her. And I don't like how you act when you're around her."

"Well, I'm not sure what you're talking about," said Leanne, sniffing and tossing her hair a lot like Cynthia. "I just know the Cravers have been very nice to me and I don't want to hear them bad-mouthed. Sam doesn't like it either."

"Okay, I hear you. I just want to find out why the fish died so we can write about it in the school paper."

"I know, but it's so stupid." Leanne opened her arms wide. "Look at this sweatshirt."

I gazed at the purple and black creation. "It's really great. Those gold threads spraying across the front look like a meteor shower."

"Yup," said Leanne, nodding, "and that's why Cayenne calls this whole collection 'Heavenly'."

"I get it."

"Okay," said Leanne, "now focus. If you look around the school, there are gobs of kids wearing Cayenne stuff."

"So?"

"So," said Leanne, her voice grim, "everyone I know cares a whole lot more about wearing great clothes than about fish."

Just then Cynthia Craver announced her entrance into the cafeteria by slamming her leather book bag on our table. Our trays were still rattling as she spoke. "I can't believe my mama didn't get me back from the dentist in time for lunch. Nothing's left except some wilted lettuce from that stupid salad bar. Leanne, give me your apple."

Leanne had been about to take a bite but she stopped and handed the apple to Cynthia. "Sure, Cyn."

I watched in total shock as Cynthia took a chomp on the big Granny Smith. How had this chick transformed my once independent friend into her slave? I was trying to figure this out when Leanne spoke. "Hey, do those jeans match my shirt?"

Cynthia pirouetted, took another bite of the apple, then struck a pose. "Are these amazing or what? They're destined to be Cayenne's next big hit. See, Emily, the design on the jeans pocket matches the one on front of Leanne's shirt—great idea, huh?"

"Nope," I replied. "The telephone was a great idea. Clothes are just clothes."

Cynthia shrugged. "When you decide to become more stylish, that cute little mall store, Daisy's, has the whole collection. Leanne, are you coming?"

Leanne nodded. "In a minute."

"Okay, I'll catch up with Sam. Talk to you later." And she was off, leaving the half-eaten apple spinning around on Leanne's tray.

Leanne finished her milk and said, "Obviously, she hasn't heard what you've been saying. When she does, it's not going to be pretty. I'm begging you to drop this crazy idea. They're just fish."

I shook my head. "Wow, you used to want to make a difference and help the world. What happened?"

"Life happened," said Leanne, picking up her lunch tray. "I keep reminding you that you have no idea what my life is like since my dad left. School is the easy part of my day. I take care of Beth after school, cook dinner most nights, and then listen to my mom bad-mouth my dad. It's depressing and exhausting to think about bad stuff all the

93

time, so I'm focusing on the football game tonight. I'm sitting in the reserved section and I hope it cools off enough for me to wear my new black Cayenne corduroy jeans so I can look cute and have some fun. Anything wrong with that?"

I started to answer, but Leanne continued. "Cynthia says nobody should be serious all the time. So, consider a little advice. Shut your mouth, ditch that story, and lighten up."

I sat rooted to the chair as Leanne flounced off. Was that the person who had been my best friend forever? She was so different now, not bad different, just someone I hardly recognized. Part of me wanted to be mad at her for ordering me around, and part of me wanted to hug her to let her know life would get better.

How could I show her I cared about her problems when it seemed she just wanted to avoid them? How was she doing this? Apparently by turning into a clone of one Cynthia Craver.

CHAPTER 14

A PICTURE IS WORTH... ?

Later, when Mom met me at the front door holding a plate of homemade sugar cookies and a glass of milk, I said, "Don't try to cheer me up. Between that snotty Cynthia and then Leanne warning me to keep my mouth shut, I've had a rotten day. I'm just glad it's over."

"Aww," said Mom, pointing the plate toward the kitchen. "Come on, I've got something you'll want to see."

I nodded, accepted the plate and glass, and trailed along after my mother. As we neared the kitchen table, Mom made a grand gesture like someone unveiling a statue. I stared at her. "Where did you get the laptop?"

"Oh, it's your dad's from work. I need to do some garden club paperwork and the desktop is acting up. So, look. These are from Aunt Sylvie. She's got bronchitis and Uncle Joe didn't want to leave her, so they e-mailed these to you."

I peered at photos on the screen. "Whoa! When did they take these?"

"Late Monday and early Tuesday morning," said Mom, with a broadening smile. "Uncle Joe wanted to figure out how to e-mail them to us. It took him until today to get the hang of it. Aunt Sylvie said there were fewer fish this time, but they're just as dead."

I frowned at the startling scenes of lifeless fish lying in the muck along the riverbank. "It *did* happen again. I wonder what Sam will say now."

"Oh, I almost forgot. You have a message to call Mary Carnell."

"Hmm, did she say what she wanted?" I asked, as I pored over the pictures.

"I think she was calling about a ride to the football game."

I scrunched my eyes shut. "Rats. I told her I'd go to *a* game with her. I didn't mean this first one. Can't you tell her I'm sick or something?"

Mom shook her head. "Absolutely not. And besides, it will do you good to get out. We're taking Ben to the dollar movie to see *Stuart Little*, so we can drop you two off on our way."

"All right, but first I need to print these out and call Sam." I grabbed the school directory, looked up Sam's number, and dialed it while swigging the last drop of milk.

Sam answered on the first ring. "Speak!"

"Hi, it's Emily."

"What's going on?"

"Are you going to the Elgin game tonight?"

"Yeah, why?" asked Sam.

"I have some photographs I want to show you."

"Well, okay, but you know Cynthia and I are kind of exclusive."

I gagged. "Dream on, big guy. These aren't pictures of me. They are sad shots of dead fish taken by my aunt and uncle earlier this week."

Sam's sigh echoed through the phone. "Em, this better be good, because it's not a welcome topic of conversation with the Cravers. It also can't take long. Cynthia and Leanne will be waiting up in the VIP section."

"Yeah, I know. Let's meet at the south stadium gate around seven. I'll be with Mary Carnell. Sam, whoever is doing this is killing a lot of fish."

Later, on the way to Mary's house, I adjusted the collar of my denim jacket and said, "I wonder if Mary owns any jeans."

"Isn't that practically a requirement for kids?" asked Dad.

"Yeah, but she's not like most kids. At least none of *my* friends. Oh, wait. I have no friends."

"Well, you have Mary," said Mom, reaching back over the seat to pat my arm. "She's a creative one from what I understand."

"Yes, she is. Here's her house, Dad. That's her in the driveway." I have to say she had on black denims, knee-high leather boots, and white sweater. Other than a neon-pink knitted shawl flung over one shoulder, she looked pretty normal.

"Hop right in the back, Mary," said Mom. "I hope you girls have enough room with Ben and his car seat between you."

"I'm fine," said Mary, as they drove toward the high school. She patted Ben's arm. "Hey, cutie. Is this a good night for football?"

"Football," answered Ben, cocking his arm like a quarterback.

I shook my head, and giggled. "Ben, you're so silly. Listen, Mary, I've got to do something before we go into the game."

Mary leaned around Ben and his car seat, and asked, "What?"

We were almost to the high school entrance. "Remember how Sam's been saying the fish dying was a one-time thing?"

"Yeah, I do."

"I've got proof he's wrong," I said, reaching for the door handle. "Dad, if by some miracle I can find a pay phone, I'll call you when it's time to come get us."

Mary ducked her head back in the car and said, "Don't worry about that. I've got my cell."

"A cell phone!" I said, loudly. "What a great idea." I nudged Mary toward the crowd surging through the south end of the stadium. A couple of kids spoke to me, and a few more stared at Mary, who was picking up litter people had dropped. Alex Johnson, whose sister was in my homeroom, hollered, "Hey, Emily, they're selling fish sticks at the concession stand!" We ignored him and kept walking until we saw Sam. He was talking to a sandy-haired man wearing a parka. When Sam saw us, he shook the man's hand and sauntered toward us.

"I just gave my first interview as editor of the school paper to Eric Timmons from the *Trib*. You two may have my autograph anytime."

I shook my head and handed Sam the photographs. He studied them for several minutes. He motioned for us to come closer. One by one he handed the pictures back to me. Mary looked on, silent, except for a few, 'Oh, mys!' Finally, Sam spoke. "Since I didn't really know you, I just assumed you were some crazy chick, and this whole fish issue was a one-time goof of nature. Apparently it's not, but it also isn't likely due to an oil spill."

"Excuse me, oil spill?"

Sam shook his head. "Never mind." He pointed to the pictures. "So, say I believe you. Now what?"

I bit my lip. "I guess I need to figure out how to get more people to listen to me."

"Right," Sam said, nodding toward the *Trib* reporter nearby. "You could give those pictures to him and let his paper run with it. But you still have no suspect."

"Well, I haven't said anything, but we've taken a few water samples along the river."

"We?" asked Sam.

"Yeah, my uncle and I. He's testing everyday."

"And?"

"Well, I'm no scientist, but at the most obvious places that might be polluting, pH, alkalinity, and temperature seemed to be normal."

"So, assuming you actually know how to test water, I repeat, you *still* have no suspect."

"Actually, she might," Mary blurted out.

"Who?" asked Sam.

Mary looked at each of us, and then spoke. "Emily asked me to make some phone calls and I talked to seven different businesses that are on the river north of Cayenne Textiles."

I felt a shiver go down my back. "And?"

"And none of them saw or had any reports of dead fish in the river near them. The dead fish only show up south of the Cayenne factory."

"Hmm," said Sam, his eyes narrowing. "And, there's nothing else around there? Like a chemical plant or a nuclear reactor?"

I shook my head. "Lakes, forests, factories, and wineries, big guy." I was sure he'd love to be the editor who saved southwest Virginia from a huge environmental disaster. He was just the type who'd jump up from the audience to accept the prize for exceptional journalism even if he never wrote a word.

"Point made," said Sam. "So, something or someone is killing fish, and lots of them."

"Yes," I said, trying not to sound too puffed up. "Let's say it's Cayenne that caused this..."

Sam's face was grim. "Say it is, you still need proof. Let me talk to my dad about what to do next."

"Your dad?"

Sam pulled his wallet from his jeans pocket and dug for something in one of the folds. He handed me a card. "Dad might not know, but he might be able to point us in the right direction."

I glanced at the business card, held it out for Mary to see, and then punched Sam's arm. "Why haven't you told us this before? Your dad is a professor of environmental studies at UVA? I could have been quizzing him about stuff all this time instead of stumbling along like a goof."

Sam sighed and grabbed the card back. "It's not what you think. He's not an environmental studies professor. He's an economist in the environmental studies *department*. He probably doesn't know a bass from a goldfish. He knows about the finances of pollution, not what causes it."

"But he's a real live professor. Can we call him now?"

"No, he's flying in tonight from some big deal conference in Chile. Just calm down. I'll talk to him and call you when I find out something. Keep quiet about this until then, okay? I don't need Cynthia to hear anything."

"Got it. I won't do anything with these pictures until I hear from you," I promised.

As we watched Sam maneuver his way through the crowd, Mary said, "I'll bet you're glad he believes you."

"Yeah, finally," I said, motioning toward the bleachers. "We'd better find seats. I've got a game to explain." I grabbed the corner of Mary's jacket and turned so fast I nearly knocked someone down.

A deep voice said, "Are you two students? Could I talk to you for a few minutes?"

I stared at the plastic badge hanging from the zipper on the man's vest. It said PRESS PASS.

CHAPTER 15
A RUDE AWAKENING

My eyes popped open. Was that the phone? What day was this? Saturday? No, that was yesterday. Ah, today was Sunday; no chores, no school. I had a speck of time before church to stretch out, enjoy the cool flutter of the sheets on my legs, and do a little uninterrupted daydreaming. Someone banged on my door. "I'm awake."

"Not good enough, young lady," said Dad, almost shouting. "Come here."

I jumped up, threw on my grey fleece robe, and flung open the door. "What's wrong? Is someone hurt?"

"No," Dad said grimly, as he unfolded the front page of the *Roanoke Tribune*. He put it about one inch from my nose. "Since when did you start giving interviews?"

I backed into my room a bit to let my eyes uncross. The headline read: *Student Hurls Dead Fish at Cayenne!* "Wow, what a headline. Can I read the rest of it?"

Dad moved around my room shaking the newspaper. "Of course you can read it. Everyone in the whole county has by now. Do you realize these are very serious accusations?"

"Dad, calm down. Eric Timmons was at the football game Friday—he's a reporter for the *Trib*."

"Yes, and here's his byline," said Dad, stabbing his finger at the paper. "So you *knew* who he was?"

"Sure," I answered. "It was really cool. He talked to me just like the high schoolers he was interviewing. He started off asking my opinion, like in a survey. Then he moved into more issue-type questions. He spoke with Mary, too."

"Yes, she's mentioned. Of course, Mary discussed Math Club and the Fall Festival, and didn't condemn one of the biggest industries in the county. *And*, she probably didn't urge kids to stop buying clothes from a company that pollutes."

"Well," I said, shoving my bare feet into my bunny slippers. "I didn't mean to condemn or accuse anyone."

"So, what *did* you mean by 'Hundreds of fish have been killed on the Higdon River and no one seems to be at fault. This seems very strange since there are lots of big businesses out there, like Cayenne Textiles.'"

"Wow, what I *said* was *something* is killing lots of fish and what if it's one of those big manufacturers on the river, like Cayenne?"

"Oh, yes, that's here, too, but then it says 'County government doesn't seem to care and just wants to take the easy way out by blaming small orchard operations instead of the big factories.'"

"Emily," said Dad, sounding like he did when he accidentally pounded his finger with a hammer, "the county government, too? Understand something here. Once words are out there, spoken, texted or e-mailed, they're out and you can't get them back."

I stared at the floor realizing he was right, but not wanting to back down. "I get it, I get it. But you *know* something's happening out on the river and I believe people should be concerned."

Dad was silent for a moment. "You're right, Em. But this article will not help your cause. And know, by tossing this idea out, you may have unfairly hurt a respected business that employs hundreds of people in this county. Not to mention, the owner of Cayenne is a very powerful man to be taking on all alone."

Mom, who stood listening at the door said, "What about the reporter? A lot of this is his fault. Why's he making such a fuss over a statement by a 13-year-old?"

"Well, apparently this reporter was clever enough to not treat our daughter like a kid," said Dad. "Emily, some reporters will do anything for a story. What he got you to say could cost us way more than just being a news item. We could be sued for a lot of money."

Suddenly, I got it. I had gotten so caught up in the "coolness" of someone listening to me, that I'd let logic fly out the window. It was a long way from a few dinky water samples that didn't even show anything to finding out who'd messed up the ecosystem of the Higdon River. "What should I do, quit?"

Dad and Mom looked at each other for a long moment, and then Dad said, "Do you have any proof to back up your accusations?"

I took a deep breath. "Not actual proof, but I'm still working on it."

"We won't make you quit just yet," said Dad. "But you have to come up with some facts soon."

"Okay, I understand. Just to let you know, all of a sudden, I have help. Mary, Sam, and now Sam's dad. He works in environmental studies at the university and he's interested in what I'm doing. I *do* need some proof to back up my big mouth so he's going to get water samples analyzed for us. I've gotten a few on my own, but now I need to get them from a couple spots further along the river, so if Mom can take us, we can get them this week."

"That's fine as long as your mother supervises, and you go nowhere near the Cayenne plant."

"Mom *supervising* us? So not necessary." I gave him a quick hug. "I'll be careful. You'll see."

After Sunday school and church services, we ate where we did most Sundays, Wilkerson's Barbecue. Hickory smoke wafted over the parking lot and followed us to our scuffed wooden table. We'd barely put our behinds on the ladder-back chair seats and got Ben in his booster chair when the waitress plunked down a wad of paper napkins, glasses of sweet tea, straws and a carton of milk. Before too many minutes she was back, spreading barbecue sandwiches, chicken, hush puppies and fries over our table. I love chicken and was polishing off the first piece when Miss June Abernathy, my third-grade teacher, stopped by our table. "I'm so sorry to interrupt. Emily, I'm proud of you for standing up for your beliefs. Keep up the good work."

Next, old Mr. Winters, who lived three doors down from us and whose son was a foreman at Cayenne, shook his cane at me. "Young lady, they've had all kinds of government testers in the plant this year. They're clean as a whistle, so mind your own business."

Watching him head out the door, Dad said, "See what you've gotten yourself into?"

I glanced around and noticed some people whispering behind their hands. I could see from their eyes if they were for or against me. I was glad when Mom tapped her watch.

Dad said, "Time to go. I think we've caused enough ruckus here."

As soon as we got home, I escaped to my room. I was rearranging my bookshelf when the phone rang. I grabbed it and said, "Hello?"

"So, you wanted to get your name in the paper too?"

"Oh, hi, Sam," I said, kind of dreading what was coming. "You're mad, right?"

"'Ya think?'" Not quite shouting, Sam went on. "You should have *told* me this yesterday when we talked about getting new water samples. I thought we agreed not to go spouting off until we had proof."

"Yeah, I got carried away. I didn't show the reporter any of the photographs, but still, I'm sorry."

"So from now on, keep a lid on things," said Sam. "Cayenne has a bunch of attorneys; who knows what they could do?"

"Like what? We're kids."

"Doesn't matter, you've alerted Cayenne we're looking at them. Now, it'll be way harder to find out the truth," said Sam. "Besides, this involves my girlfriend's father, who happens to be on Cayenne's board of directors and runs the company."

"I know," I agreed. "That's the bad part of living in a small town. Hey, we're still going for water samples Wednesday, right?"

There was a really long pause.

"Sam?"

Finally, he answered. "I'm thinking. Again, this is dealing with my girlfriend's father, plus I know Cynthia's whole family. They've sort of taken me under their wing."

"Yeah, they seem to be good at that."

Sam said, "Well, they're very generous people. Her dad's given me so much soccer gear and all kinds of free tickets to things. And Cynthia's so pretty and funny." A long sigh came through the phone.

I remembered something my dad had said at lunch. "Listen, about the samples. I can't go unless my mom takes us."

"Are you serious? What are we, babies?" groaned Sam. "I thought we would just ride our bikes."

"Hey, at first my parents weren't going to let me do it at all. They're freaked out by thoughts of me getting arrested."

"That makes sense. Listen, it won't take as long if she drives us," said Sam. "But remind her we don't want to get there until after the plant closes."

"Um, here's the deal. As far as my parents know, we're just getting samples in the vicinity and we have to go that late 'cuz you have soccer practice all week. We don't mention the part about our feet actually touching factory property. We need flashlights in case we're out after dark, and you're bringing more official-looking containers for the water."

"All right, listen. I need to think about this whole thing a little more. Can you call me back later?"

"No problem," I said. "Just remember, you're editor of the school paper. Do you really just want us to write about bake sales and school dances? Aren't you curious about what's going on? Or are you the kind of editor who can be bought off with soccer gear?"

All I heard was a click and silence. *Okay, Sam, I'll call you back.*

"Em," called Dad from the hallway. "Leanne on your mom's cell."

"Did you say Leanne?" I asked, opening my bedroom door. I tossed the house phone on my bed and grabbed the cell. "Hey, how'd you get my mom's number?"

"She gave it to me when I spent the night in case I ever needed her," shouted Leanne. "And, though I love talking to *her*, I'm probably never speaking to you again."

"Whoa, Leanne. What is wrong with you?"

"I can't believe you contacted the newspaper and bothered someone at the university with some stupid story about six or seven dead fish."

"Hey, I didn't 'contact' the newspaper. The reporter was at the game talking to tons of other kids. And, I haven't even met Sam's dad yet, but he seems interested mostly because it's hundreds of dead fish, not six or seven. *And*, I didn't say anything about the university. How do you know all this?"

"Well, everyone's read the paper. Sam told Cynthia about his dad getting involved. She is so mad she ordered him to print something about it in the school paper, like you overstepped your authority to speak. She's popular, Em. Don't be surprised if kids aren't speaking to you. I'm done with this and you. Goodbye!"

The line went dead just as Mom tapped on the door. "Em? Is she okay? Is she coming over?"

"Yup, she's okay, but I don't think she'll be coming over anytime soon. She hates me."

"Leanne could never hate you," Mom said, standing in the hall, sipping some coffee.

I grabbed my homework from my book bag. "Well, I guess the phones have been lighting up. Apparently, it's not a popular idea that I want to know what killed the fish. It seems weird. If they don't care if the fish died, why do they care if I'm asking questions?"

"Well, maybe it's not what you say, but how you say it. Sometimes you tend to blurt stuff out."

"Thanks for that vote of confidence, Mom."

"Sorry. But, you've really got to start watching what you're saying. I doubt you'll be winning many favorite girl of the year contests with this thing. Are you sure you know how to handle yourself?"

"Mom, I *know* this is a big deal. I don't want to quit now. I don't think you trust me to follow through, but you might want to start. Face it, I'm not a little kid anymore." I took a deep breath. "Now, I have to study."

Then, I did something I'd never done before. I shut the door in my mom's face.

CHAPTER 16
THE HUNT BEGINS

Returning home after a quiet Labor Day cookout with my grandparents, we found a huge black garbage bag swinging from our mailbox pole near the edge of our yard. My dad pulled the car in the driveway and parked, and we all got out. He said, "Wait here."

We watched as he untied the bag from the mailbox, looked it over, pulled off something that was taped to the front of the bag, and then motioned to us. Ben, Mom, and I hurried over, hoping it was something really cool. It wasn't. Someone had gone to a lot of trouble to leave a bag of coffee grounds, smashed pumpkins, wet leaves, and a faint whiff of manure. The gift tag my dad had removed said 'Fight This Pollution, Little Girl'.

My mom gasped and said, "Emily, take Ben in the house. Someone might be watching us."

I looked at Dad and lifted up my hands, like "What do I do?"

Dad took my little brother's hand and said, "Come on, Ben, let's put this garbage where it belongs, in the trash. Em, talk to your mother and convince her why you should continue on this quest for fish killers."

It took a half hour of me reminding my mom how she and my dad protested wars and stood up for voters' rights in college before she calmed down enough to say, "Go to your room. I've had all I can take of doing the right thing for today."

I trudged upstairs and stretched out on my bed to do some reading for English. Not too much later, the phone in my room rang, ending my efforts to concentrate on sonnets. I grabbed the receiver, and said, "Hello."

"Emily, it's Mary."

"Oh, hi," I said, flopping across my bed. "Did you have a good day off?"

"No, we had to go to a big deal art show for my dad down in Atlanta this weekend, and we just got back. I saw the newspaper article. My parents thought it was great."

I giggled. "Well, sure, that was because you talked to the reporter about normal school things. *My* parents had a fit because I shouldn't have blabbed my opinions."

"Ouch," sympathized Mary. "The article did make you sound kind of controversial."

"Hmm, I've definitely agitated some people. Someone gave us a huge bag of smelly garbage, for free! They left it tied to our mailbox, and left a sign saying, 'Fight This Pollution, Little Girl'."

"Wow, that's scary."

"Yeah, my mom was freaked. Part of me was too. But, mostly it just made me more determined to keep on with this. Weirdly, Sam's agreed to help me. Wednesday we're going to get water samples. Mr. Wheeler said we need them from above the Cayenne plant and below."

"I can come with you. Maybe it would go quicker if we spread out."

"Sounds good." I was thankful for Mary's help, because except for the newspaper meetings, I didn't really know Sam that well. "Be sure and bring a flashlight and some bug spray."

"Got it," replied Mary. "Hey, did Sam's dad say what he thought might be happening to the fish?"

"Yeah, he's checking something called fish fry."

"Was he joking?"

"It's not really funny. Apparently, if a textile factory doesn't cool the dye water before it's dumped into the river it could rob the oxygen from the water so either the temperature kills the fish or they can't breathe. Pick one, but it still equals dead fish."

"Gee," murmured Mary, "I never figured you for such a brain."

"Yeah, most people think I'm just a jock because of swim team."

"I know what you mean. People never figure me to be an athlete."

I choked down a laugh. "An athlete?"

"Uh-huh," said Mary. "I compete in balance beam for the 'Y' team."

"Do you practice a lot?"

"Yup, three times a week. Hopefully, the high school will have a team by the time we're freshmen."

"Wow, who knew? See ya tomorrow." I hung up thinking how nice Mary was, and really not nerdy like everyone said. I used to talk like this with Leanne. But that was the old Leanne B.C., before Cynthia.

~

As I stuffed my lunch in my backpack Tuesday morning, Mom gave me a solemn look. "I'm sorry I sounded like I doubted you the other day, kiddo. I was just worried, and even more so after what we found on our mailbox."

I shrugged. "I know, that was creepy. But, Mom, think about it. Pollution, if that's it, is bad enough alone, but what if someone's lying and getting away with it? That's cheating." I sprinted to the bus just in time to hop on board. As I walked down the aisle, there was a silence in the air that gave me the shivers. It felt like those days when an ice storm hits during school and Mrs. Randall, our driver, has to keep the huge yellow beast from sliding off the edge of the earth. I felt everyone's eyes staring at me.

When I went to plop into my favorite seat, Robby Brown said, "Sorry, I'm saving this one."

I looked around, but no one budged. I ended up on the little side seat in the far back of the bus, next to a box of oily rags. Only the dorky kids sat back here or the ones who smelled bad. I tried to study my math notes, but I couldn't concentrate. Once, when the bus was stopped at the railroad crossing, I caught Mrs. Randall glancing at me in the rearview mirror. She was always so jolly, but now she was scowling. Then I remembered. Mrs. Randall's husband was a foreman at the Cayenne plant. Gosh, all this because of a few questions about fish?

The answer became clear when I got to school. A dead goldfish hung on the handle of my locker. Taped to the door was a note: "Too Late, Em, I Can't Be Saved!!!! Signed, C.C.". Half the school seemed to be standing around waiting for my reaction. I peeled off the note and tossed it in the nearest trashcan. The crowd began to buzz like the middle of a hornet's nest. I carefully untied the fish, wrapped it in a tissue, and gave it to an innocent little sixth-grader. "This needs to go to Cyn Craver in Homeroom #14."

CHAPTER 17

SINK OR SWIM

After our early supper Wednesday, Mom took us out to the river. "We'll meet you at Aunt Sylvie's in about an hour," I said. "Remember, some of us have cell phones. Plus, everyone has a flashlight if it gets dark while we're out. Bye." She'd dropped us at the boat ramp upriver from the Cayenne plant. In one hand, I carried the small box of jars that Sam had brought, and with the other, I pointed the way. The jars were from the university and reminded me of Ben's baby food jars, but with extra rubber liners in the lids to keep contamination out. They also had official-looking labels that made them look very big deal compared to my recycled canning jars. Mary clomped along beside me, her combat boots alerting every deer in the forest to our approach. "Remind me why you're wearing those boots?"

"I didn't want to step on any snakes."

"I don't think that's a problem," I said. "They'll hear you and slither away for their lives."

Sam had a backpack slung over one shoulder and munched an apple as he followed behind us. "Forget her, Mary. She's just grumpy about dead fish in her locker. I'm glad you came to help."

We followed the path the power company had cut through the woods. As dry orange and red leaves crunched under our feet, Mary pulled her camouflage vest tighter. "It's weird out here. No houses, no cars."

"It does feel like we're in the boonies," agreed Sam. "But the factory where they made my bedroom furniture is about a half-mile upriver from here, so we're not that far from civilization."

"Yeah, you're right." I said. "Hey, Sam, did you tell Cynthia what we're doing?"

"Are you kidding? If the Craver family knew I was with 'the enemy'..."

"Me?"

"Bingo," said Sam. "If she finds out, you can pretty much figure I'll be girlfriendless."

I wasn't sure how serious having a girlfriend in middle school was. This type of thing was out of my league, but I did feel kind of bad. When Sam wasn't showing off, he was actually a decent type of guy. "Sorry," I said.

"Ah, don't be. Part of me wanted to help you from the beginning." He paused. "When I was ten or eleven, my dad took a leave from his job to help clean up at an oil spill in the Gulf. My mom was on some big projects, so they had me go with him for a few weeks to help."

"Did you go out in boats?" I asked.

He shook his head. "I was too young, so we had to stay on shore. We cleaned up sea birds, gulls, terns, and ducks. It was awful."

"Awful?" asked Mary. "You were helping."

"I know. But, you looked into the eyes of those birds and you knew, even though you got every speck of oil, they might not survive. When Em showed me those photos, the first things I saw were those eyes. They seem to follow you. I couldn't ignore them, I guess. So here I am."

"Wow, thanks. Apparently, that makes three of us, the eyes." The path ended at a place on the river that looked like it was on a postcard for a trout stream. Rippling water flickered with bits of the setting sun. Leaves, some still green, others the color of pumpkins and harvest corn, floated along like boats. It was so quiet, it felt like we should whisper. I handed Sam a jar. "So, you've done this sampling thing before?"

"Not exactly." Sam dropped in the floating thermometer and swished the jar through the water, careful not to scrape bottom. He squinted at the sample in the fading light. "I've tested drinking water and compared it to sterilized water for purity, stuff like that. That was for a science project, so I'm guessing it's not much different." He grabbed the thermometer and noted the water temp.

"Makes sense," said Mary, peeking over his shoulder. "Can you tell anything by looking at it?"

He shook his head. "Not really, unless you've got a fresh source of pollution. Then you see particles or random colors that you know don't belong there." He twisted the lid on, handed the jar and a marker to Mary who labeled it "Sample #1 Boat Ramp Sept. 5", and zipped it into one of the pockets on her vest.

Sam tapped his watch and said, "We've got to get moving."

Thanks to the dry summer, many trees had already dropped their leaves. This helped us spot the Cayenne plant through the woods. We tromped back along a different path, dodging trees, thick tangles of bushes, and vines. We came out of the woods onto the road near the front entrance of Cayenne. Dusk was approaching, giving everything a shadowy gloom. "Sam, I'm thinking we get one sample right here at the factory, then two more downstream."

"Did you say at the factory?" Mary's mouth dropped open. "You told your mom we weren't going to trespass on the Cayenne property."

I put up my hand. "Quiet. I know what I told her. But we're here and we should try to get this sample. Cayenne doesn't own the river."

"She's right, Mary," said Sam, "Once we get in the river, the water is free to anyone."

Free, maybe. Easy, not so much. A towering chain-link fence reaching all the way down into the river greeted us with imposing warning signs posted in red and black letters: "PRIVATE PROPERTY! CAYENNE TEXTILES! KEEP OUT!"

Mary giggled nervously. "Are we going over the fence?"

I looked at Sam and shrugged. "Not if we can find another way in. Otherwise, yes."

"Right," agreed Sam. "Let's get in, get the sample, and get out of here."

"Come on," I urged. Pushing against the fence, we moved inland and tried over and over to find a loose section. It took longer than we'd planned. Finally, at one spot, the fence gave way from its support pole. I set the box down, wiggled through the opening, and whispered, "Next?"

Ignoring the opening, Sam climbed up and over the fence. Landing on the soft dirt beside me, he made a grand bow.

"Impressive," I said, laughing softly, yet thinking, *Okay, he's still Sam.* "Mary, can you slip me a jar through the fence?" I looked around a minute to fix the entry point in my mind. Then I grabbed the jar from Mary. "Stay here and have a story ready."

"Story?"

Sam nodded. "She's right. If a security guy comes along, tell him your dog is lost out here somewhere."

Mary looked toward the woods. "All right. Lost dog, I got it. Just hurry, I'm no nature person, it's spooky out here, and it's way darker than I thought. Plus, I'm guessing if we're not at your aunt's pretty soon, your mom will come barreling after us."

"And I will be so busted if she does," I muttered.

"Let's go," Sam urged.

I took off, following the sound of rushing water. We cut across a small parking lot marked "Office Personnel" and slipped past a loading dock to the rear of the factory. Fifty more steps to the riverbank. We'd made it! I handed Sam a jar and the thermometer. He squatted, put the thermometer in, did his swishing thing through the water, capped the jar, marked it "Sample #2 C.T. Sept.5", and slipped it into his backpack. We made no sound as we waited for the thermometer to reach the same temp as the water. As soon as it made it, I grabbed it, Sam recorded it in our notes, and just as we started back, we heard footsteps moving toward us. A light, bright enough to make us squint, flashed in our faces, freezing us into place.

"Didn't you kids see the signs?" growled a uniformed man holding the spotlight. His voice reminded me of a gangster movie.

Shading my eyes, I blurted out, "Yes, sir, we saw the signs, but my dog ran off and we thought he might have headed this way."

"Seems to be a lot of that," he said, motioning toward the parking lot. "Supposing we mosey back the way you came in and see if your friend has found *her* dog yet."

"Sure, sir," said Sam, speaking up. "Of course, we're all looking for the same dog. It's actually kind of funny."

The man lowered the spotlight, and squinted hard at us. "I don't think trespassing is funny, son."

"No, sir."

Raising the spotlight again, the guard asked, "What's in the backpack?"

Sam pulled the pack off his shoulder, unzipped it and opened it up to show the guard. "A couple apples, and a marker, sir. Oh, and some water in the outside pocket."

I nodded and tried to sound earnest. "Um, it's water for my dog."

"Doesn't seem like much water for a dog unless he's a runt." The guard took a step toward me. "You young folks from around here?"

"Well, I was born here. We all live in town, sir."

The guard beamed the light full force on my face.

I couldn't speak, feeling so woozy I thought I'd faint. Sweat trickled down my back like little spiders dancing on my spine. I wondered what they did to trespassers.

The guard snapped his two-way radio from his belt. "John, I got intruders here. North river side. One of them is a girl. I'm thinkin' it might be that one the boss warned us about. I'm bringing them in. Meet me in Lot A."

I looked at Sam, and a silent message flashed between us. Run! We took off. The security guard lunged at me, grabbing the hoodie I'd tied around my waist. The knot let go leaving him holding an empty shirt. We hauled out and Sam reached the parking lot first. He shot across it and edged along the fence. "Mary, where are you?"

Behind him, I gasped, "I'm going to puke."

"Deep breath," ordered Sam, instantly taking charge of our mission. "Get over the fence. That guy's coming."

I yelled, "And another one."

Sam glanced at the security patrol car speeding across the parking lot. "Come on."

I frantically pushed at the fence looking for our escape spot.

Mary blinked her flashlight at us, tugged on a corner of the fence, and held it open while Sam and I slipped through. Shouting loudly, the guard aimed the spotlight straight at us. I spun around to pick up the box of empty jars I'd left by the fence. The second guard leaped from the car and joined his partner in the chase. The slapping sounds of their feet made me jump and drop the box. I reached for it but Sam waved me off and grabbed two jars with his free hand. Mary called, "This way."

We followed Mary as she turned sharply and ducked into the woods. The guards were climbing over the fence. I yelled, "Keep going, Mary," as we followed her light along a zigzag course around trees and bushes.

The ground was uneven and I struggled with my footing as we raced up a steep incline. When we finally reached the crest, I motioned for everyone to stop. All I could hear was my own heart pounding and Mary's gaspy breathing.

Sam whispered, "Think we lost them, Em?"

"No idea. Just keep moving."

Sam nodded. "Which way is south?"

Mary dug into her pocket and brought out a small object. She aimed her light over it, peered for a moment, then looked up and pointed. "South, this way."

I plowed ahead, and Mary and Sam fell in behind. I turned my head to avoid a branch, and asked, "Mary, where'd you get the compass?"

Mary giggled. "I was a Girl Scout."

"You?"

"What can I say?" said Mary. "I liked the crafts."

CHAPTER 18
NOWHERE TO HIDE

Since Mary, with her magic compass, could point us in the right direction, we plowed ahead.

"Gosh," I muttered, as river mud squished over the sides of my shoes, "this is nasty."

"Just keep moving," warned Sam. "Those guards could still be tracking us."

I slogged on, thinking about the two people behind me. Sam had dropped his whole surfer attitude and now was acting way more mature than he ever did in school. When had this happened? I'd been so wrapped up in myself, the fish, and Leanne, I'd barely noticed how the world and the people around me were changing. Before today, I would have sworn Mary was basically afraid of everything, but she seemed so excited to be a part of this.

"Just thought I'd let you two know, I recognize these woods. When I was little, I used to play along here with Leanne. We built forts, climbed trees, that kind of silly stuff." I sighed and picked up my pace, dodging low-hanging pine branches as I went. "The Pittsboro boat ramp is just ahead. Let's make a quick stop and get the third sample there and the fourth at Aunt Sylvie's. I just hope this all hasn't been a colossal waste of time."

"What if it has?" asked Sam, as we arrived at the boat landing. "You take a chance when you're trying to prove something. So let's test this and raise the odds."

Mary dug into a pocket and produced a plastic bag full of trail mix. She opened it and held it out to me. "Not many boaters here tonight. Do you think the guards gave up?"

I munched granola, grateful for the occasional dried banana or piece of chocolate, and watched Sam snag the water sample. "I have no idea about the guards. I'm just hoping they don't report us. Either way, I'm probably in big trouble with my mom."

Mary nodded. "I could be, too. I've gotta be home before nine. It's a school night."

"Don't remind me," I said. "Come on, Aunt Sylvie's is just around the next bend. The water's high along here. Our feet are going to be beyond soggy."

"Who cares about soggy feet?" Sam grumbled. "All I've had to eat is that apple. It's way past my dinnertime and I'm ready to roll on home. Here's the sample. Let's get out of here."

I tugged on Mary's sleeve and we plunged ahead. I breathed in the faint aroma of smoke. "Smell that?"

"Yeah," said Mary. "Do you think there's a fire?"

"Yup, right where one's supposed to be, in my aunt's fireplace," I said, pointing. Smoke drifted from the chimney of the little log house. Lights glowed through the window and from party bulbs strung on wires along the boat dock, reflecting in the rippling water of the river.

"It's like a doll house," exclaimed Mary.

"I told you, it's one of my favorite places."

"Wow, nice spot," murmured Sam.

"It is," I agreed. "Except when the riverbank is covered with rotting fish."

Uncle Joe came out of the house and headed down to meet us. "I heard on my police scanner there was trouble at the Cayenne plant. You three know anything about that?"

I scooped my arm through his and said, "Uncle Joe, do we look like troublemakers?"

"No," he admitted, "but I'm guessing at least one of you was trespassing."

"Maybe two, sir," said Sam. "But it was for a good cause."

Uncle Joe threw his other arm around Sam. "Son, if it will stop heaps of dead perch from showing up in my yard, I'm sure it was."

Ben came trotting along waving a flashlight. "I'm helping, Em."

Sam shielded the light beam with his hand and said, "You sure are. Your name's Ben, right? Will you help me?" He grabbed Ben's hand and they walked to the end of Uncle Joe's dock and lay down on their bellies. Sam directed Ben's hand with the flashlight in it to a spot on the water where Sam kept his arm underwater quite a while. I held onto the string attached to the thermometer, submerged it, and we waited. Finally, Sam scooped up the sample, and I hauled in the thermometer. Ben aimed the flashlight so we could write some info in our notes. Then Sam let Ben help cap the jar, and we started up the hill.

Aunt Sylvie and Mom waited on shore. The women were each carrying a camping lantern. Mom held hers high and it reflected the worry on her face. "Emily, are you three all right? I expected you here long before now. I was about to jump in my car to hunt you down."

I was going to answer when the sound of heavy footsteps on the crushed gravel path made me look around. Staring hard at me was a tall man in full uniform including a gun in his holster. The chunky face of our county sheriff, Maynard Johnson, glowed in the lantern light. His deputy stood several feet back. "Evening, folks," said the sheriff, moving closer to me. "You are Emily Sanders, correct?"

Mom stepped forward and said, "She is, but why are you asking?"

The sheriff held up his hand as if to shush Mom, and then gazed at my mud-crusted shoes. "Been wade-fishing, Emily?"

I shook my head, and even though my mouth was as dry as if I'd been chewing gravel, said, "No, sir."

"I didn't think so. Are these your friends?"

I introduced Mary, who stared at the ground, and Sam, who suddenly acted like he was a travel agent.

"Pleased to meet you, sir," Sam said. "I've just moved here and Emily was showing us around. It's a beautiful area out here on the river, a great place to skip stones and hike. We've even been working on our science projects."

"That so?" asked the sheriff, turning back to me. "Young lady, your little river tour sounds interesting, but I'm out here for a different purpose. I'm not sure if your mother knows this or not, but we have reason to believe you've been trespassing on Cayenne Textile property."

Mom's mouth dropped open. "Emily was trespassing? What makes you think that?"

"We had reports from the security crew at the Cayenne plant about two kids climbing fences."

I buried my first reaction of spilling my guts and went with something unlike me, smart-alecky and stubborn. I said, "Well, I wasn't climbing any fences and Sam told you what we've been doing."

Sheriff Johnson reached back for something his deputy was holding out. "You always go hiking with a box of jars?"

I saw the mailing label stuck on the cardboard box. Sam's parents' names were on it. He'd said his grandma had sent Mom and Dad an anniversary gift in that box. My armpits moistened as I realized how little time it took to go from cocky to confessing. "Sir, we were gathering water samples to find out if Cayenne Textiles is polluting the river."

"That's what Mr. Craver said they might be doing," said the deputy.

"Emily, you promised," said Mom. "Please tell me you didn't do this."

Somehow my vocal cords seemed locked. Everything I'd done recently came crashing down on me, and I thought, *Am I this stupid? Getting in big trouble for fish? What an idiot!*

Sam cleared his throat. "It's pretty much my fault. I told her the sampling wouldn't be complete without one at the plant."

The sheriff pulled some papers from his hip pocket and made notes while everyone stood silent. When he finished, he raised his arm and clicked his pen as if to call us to attention. "Gathering samples or whatever you want to call it is *still* trespassing, and charges may be filed."

"Charges?" asked Mom.

Sheriff Johnson snapped the sheaf of papers in the air. "Mr. Craver dictated a statement to us a short while ago. It says, 'I will not bring a complaint of trespassing against Emily Sanders and accomplices if she agrees to a public apology to my family and the Cayenne employees.'"

Wow, how could anybody get something like that done in what, a nanosecond? Dad was right. Mr. Craver was a powerful man. I swallowed and found my voice. "An apology?"

The sheriff went on. "It says your accusations and insinuations have damaged his company's reputation."

That didn't sound good. Still, something prickled inside me not to let this go. "Sir," I said, "what happens if I can prove those accusations?"

Sheriff Johnson stared at me. "Mr. Craver has given you until Friday of next week at 4:00 p.m. to come up with an apology. Seems more than fair to me, so use your time wisely. This apology will take place at your school."

Mom shook his hand. "We'll be there, Sheriff."

"Great," said Sheriff Johnson, tipping his hat. "Don't forget, parents are accountable for their children's actions in this county. Evening, folks." He and the deputy strode off through the night.

No one spoke for a moment. Then I said, "Mom, what did he mean, accountable for their actions?"

Mom's face lined with worry. "It means we could be sued for who knows how much."

CHAPTER 19

FACTS DON'T LIE

Saturday afternoon, I looked up and squinted at Mary, who was seated across the kitchen table from me. Would she come visit us in jail if Sam and I got arrested for trespassing? Would what we did eventually get her in trouble, too? She was, after all, our accomplice, and possibly guilty by association. Poor kid, if only... "Huh?"

Mary lifted her math book. "I asked how you did number eleven."

"I'm sorry. I should be concentrating on our math homework, right?" I tapped my pencil. "It's Saturday. We got those water samples three days ago and not one word from Sam." I sighed.

"It'll be okay," said Mary, nodding. She pointed to the heap of papers in front of me. "Find any new information about pollution?"

I shrugged. "Yeah, heaps. Unfortunately nothing I can use. I'm thirsty. Want something?"

Just then, the telephone rang. I jumped up, grabbed the cordless handset, and started toward the refrigerator. I stopped in the middle of the kitchen. "You've got to be kidding, Sam."

Mary glanced up and whispered, "What's wrong?"

I held up my hand, and said, "Hey, hold on a minute. Mary's here. I'm gonna put you on speakerphone so we all can talk."

Sam cleared his throat. "Can you hear me?"

I stomped impatiently. "You're coming in loud and clear. What's the deal with the water samples?"

Sam's sigh filled the kitchen. "I checked all the samples and my dad rechecked them when he got in today. The water doesn't change significantly from above the plant to below. In fact, one sample was so pure, you could drink it."

I slumped into a kitchen chair. "I can't believe this. I was so sure." I pawed frantically through my research folders. "Sam, what about temperature? Remember, I found in my research that if the water a textile plant uses isn't cooled enough when it's dumped back into a river or lake, it can rob fish and creatures of oxygen?"

"Right, I asked my dad about that. It happens a lot. Or used to."

"So, what's different now?"

Sam cleared his throat again. "Like I said, it might have been a problem years ago, but Cayenne has one of the most sophisticated cooling devices around. In fact, my dad's research team helped design the original."

Mary spoke up. "Sam, one time during a newspaper staff meeting Emily asked you about the dyes. Anything there?"

"Um, the way I understand it is, blues and greens can cause some problems. Metal particles, junk like that. But the water we got was clear of everything except a little tree bark. Sorry."

"Hey," I said, "what if they just don't happen to be running blue and green this week? Think about it. Nobody's ever mentioned timing. I don't think we can ignore the dye thing."

Sam sighed. "You are relentless, but it's a good point. I'll ask. I'm sure he's thought of it, but I'll check."

"Okay, one more thing," I said, feeling like a dog with a bone. "What about the sample you took on Aunt Sylvie's dock? Wasn't that going to be for dissolved oxygen?"

"What's that?" asked Mary.

"Fish, and other water stuff like crabs or worms, need oxygenated water to breathe. Like you've seen stagnant ponds in the dead of summer, with still water or tons of stuff growing in it?"

"Right," agreed Sam, "so lots of times if there's not enough dissolved oxygen, fish die. Emily tested for it with the samples from the golf course and the saw mill. Those tests were fine." He sighed. "The sample we got the other night? No problem in the Higdon, as least now. The water's moving fast, it's cooler out, so the numbers were good."

"Did you tap the bottle?"

"Yes, Miss Science pro," said Sam, starting to sound grumpy. "No trapped air bubbles in the jars, even though it was all but dark when we got those samples."

Mary laughed, and said, "You two crack me up. I never expected all this from a swimmer and a surfer."

"Yeah, thanks," I said. "I guess we shouldn't be surprised. We have clean water and no fish are dying right now. Those are supposed to be good things." I shrugged. "That's it then. I'll have to apologize after all. Thanks anyway, Sam. Sorry for wasting your time."

"No problem. It takes care of the whole girlfriend issue. See you at school Monday."

I sat, ignoring the dial tone sounding through the speaker. Finally, Mary shut it off. "Do you want to do any more math problems?"

I shook my head. "I'll call you tomorrow when I finish them. I feel like such a fool. Who was I to think I could take on a big company and prove they were industrial polluters?"

"Well, I think you were very brave," said Mary, as she gathered her books and jacket. "Something still could show up."

I laughed. "Yeah, if a dump truck full of toxic waste falls from the sky."

Mary slipped out the back door. I watched until she got to the corner, and then shut the door on the day. I'd let everyone down. And now I had to write an apology to Cynthia Craver's father and all his employees. I bit my lip. Apologies were supposed to come from the heart. Right now, my heart felt squeezed out like a used-up sponge. And definitely not apologetic.

CHAPTER 20
SOMETHING'S FISHY

Early Sunday morning, I watched the clock, hoping to hear the sound of Dad's car in the driveway before Mom, Ben, and I left for church. I'd written the apology to Mr. Craver, and it sat on the counter, mocking me. It was right beside a phone message from Leanne saying, "Call me sometime." I turned away so I couldn't see either one of them. I still had a few math problems to finish, but I needed help. Mom loved words, not numbers, and never offered help for math homework. Dad would help, but I'd have to wait. He'd been called in to work overtime on a malfunctioning computer and had been there all night. I was staring out the window at the sun rising over the trees in the backyard when the phone rang. "Hello?"

Uncle Joe's gravelly voice said, "Sorry to call so early, Emily, but Fiona got loose this morning and the craziest thing happened."

I waited for him to go on. Pet goat stories usually took a long time to tell. "Was she chasing the cat again?"

"That's probably how it started. She tore through the yard, pulled down the clothesline and almost ran up the ladder that was leaning against the shed. When that didn't work, she took off for the river and got her horns caught in the hammock."

I smiled. What a storyteller. "And then?"

"Well, I tied her up and put her back in the pen," said Uncle Joe. There was silence on the line for a moment. Then he spoke. "I think you may want to come out here real soon."

I felt a chill go down my spine. "Why?"

"When I caught up with Fiona, she was poking her nose in about half a dozen dead fish."

"Are you serious? Did they look recently dead or real dead?"

He chuckled. "Good thing I understand how the females on your side of the family speak. These fish appear to have just croaked. No bulging guts, just glassy-eyed creatures floating belly-up."

"Uncle Joe, I've been thinking about something. It's probably stupid, but I was wondering if they work weekends or midnight shifts at the Cayenne plant."

"Not usually," he said. "But it's funny you should mention it. A few nights here lately there have been *buses* rumbling down the road. The first time I heard it, I figured they were tour buses that got lost coming off the highway. Yesterday, I heard them again, and then again quite a few hours later, going in the other direction. They could have been at Cayenne, but they could have been going to an event on the river just as easily. It's odd, though, to have bus traffic around here so often."

I thought a moment. The plant wasn't operating a second shift when we got the water samples. No workers, no dead fish. Now, dead fish and buses? There was probably no connection, but I still needed new water samples. "Uncle Joe, I might try and get out there today."

"We'll be around," said Uncle Joe. "I'd best be cleaning up those fish. Bye now."

"Bye." I clicked the phone and quickly dialed Sam, hoping it wasn't too early to call. "Feel like a bike ride?"

"Nope, I feel like thirty more minutes of sleep. I've got a club soccer game at 11:00."

"Sorry, but I really need you to meet me at the corner of Highway 9 and Milton Marine at two o'clock."

"Why?"

"We've got to get out to the river again."

"Aw, Emily, after soccer, I've got homework to do. And a yard to rake."

"Okay, I know you're busy, so how about three? We've got to get another water sample."

"Again? Why?"

"More fish have died."

He groaned. "All right, I'll be there, but I'm not going to say anything about it to my dad yet. He's pretty much given up on this whole pollution idea."

"Okay, I understand. Please, just come."

Later, as we pedaled down Highway 9, I asked, "Do you like living here better than Greensboro?"

Sam shook his head. "The people are nice, but there isn't much going on. It's kind of hard to adjust 'cause it's like the smallest place I've ever lived."

"You've moved around a lot?"

"Yeah, I was born in Michigan, and then we moved to California. That's where my mom is from and I've got lots of relatives there. Then we moved to Houston, then Greensboro and now here. This is about half-way between my parents' jobs. Dad's up at the university and Mom's a freelance furniture designer. She works for some of the factories here and down in North Carolina, so this is convenient for her, too."

"Wow, what a different life. My whole family, both sides, is from here." We passed a red brick house, trimmed in dark green shutters perched up on a little hill. There were some people getting out of a car. The car horn honked and I waved. "Cousins. Got 'em all over the county."

"Guess if you ever do something bad everyone knows in a flash."

I shook my head as we turned off on the road to the plant. "Please. I've always been the 'good girl'. You know, the one who carries the teacher's lunch down to the school refrigerator. My worst offense ever was I threw salt at a boy in the cafeteria once because he called me 'Red Riding Hood.' I got detention and there were already four phone calls to my parents by the time I got home."

"Man, this fish thing must be driving your family crazy."

I nodded as we bumped along a dirt shortcut trail through the woods at the edge of the Cayenne property. "Yeah, they've got neighbors and friends who work for Cayenne. I've riled some of them up, that's for sure. Not to mention my parents. If we get caught today, I won't be grounded for just a month, it'll be for the rest of my life!"

We got off our bikes and pushed them along the fence surrounding the factory. I stopped, unzipped my backpack and pulled out a camera.

Sam asked, "You going to take a picture of the building?"

"Well, no. I wanted to come out here for water samples, but also because of something my Uncle Joe said."

"What's that?"

"He said there'd been buses going up and down this road."

Sam pulled some shrubbery branches aside and pointed, "Like those?"

I glanced toward the Cayenne parking lot and did a double take. There were dozens of people coming out of the factory. I aimed the camera and snapped a few shots. "They're carrying lunch boxes and jackets. Think they're workers?"

Sam shrugged. "I could ask Cynthia."

"Be serious." I turned and quietly said, "I have this crazy, weird feeling."

"Aliens from another planet weird? I'm not sure why we should care about random overtime workers," said Sam, motioning me to get my bike.

I could tell he wanted to get this over with. "Okay, sorry to let my imagination run wild. Let's get those water samples, from the legal side of the fence this time. Then we'll go on to Aunt Sylvie's."

I lowered the thermometer in and we waited. Then he scooped a water sample and passed it over to me. I started to put it in my backpack, then squinted at it for several seconds. "Sam, you'd better look at this."

He shrugged. "Okay, but the river's not muddied up here."

I stared at the water lapping at the tips of my tennis shoes. I could see sticks and pebbles scattered on the river bottom so clearly it was as if I'd held them in my hand. "I know the river looks pristine, low turbidity and all that, but this sample doesn't."

"What?" he asked, as he grabbed for the jar. He was quiet for a long moment, then whistled. "This is amazing."

"I thought so," I said, pulling up the thermometer and trying not to sound too triumphant. "What do you think is in there?"

"Definitely specks of something that wasn't there the last time."

"Bad specks? Or maybe just tree bark or dirt?"

Sam shook his head. "I don't think so, even though that stuff's there, too."

I got down on my knees, ignoring the mud oozing onto my jeans. "It's clear on top, but about halfway down, there's junk floating."

Sam squatted beside me. "I bet anything that junk is metal particles. I'm gonna grab one more sample, then let's get down to your aunt's place."

We pedaled furiously. The setting sun's pink and peachy rays glowed from behind a small sprinkling of clouds. I wrinkled my nose, and said, "I could tell we're here even if I were blindfolded. Except now the amazing smell of the apple orchard is mingled with the disgusting odor of rotting fish."

Sam nodded grimly as we walked our bikes down toward the riverbank in front of Aunt Sylvie's.

Uncle Joe came from the back of the shed. "Hi there, kids. I had a wheelbarrow full of fish by the time I was through. I took a couple more instant photos to show what a mess it was. You two here for more water?"

I reached for the snapshots, and nodded. "We may have something this time." We watched as Sam strode to the end of the dock and got the sample. When he stood up and examined the jar, a big smile spread across his face. "More particles?" I asked.

He nodded. "Many more. I can't wait for my dad to see this. He had been thinking the problem might be *Pfisteria*."

Uncle Joe and I looked at each other. I said, "Huh?"

Sam walked toward us. "It's an organism that's been attacking fish and stuff in North Carolina and it's moved into Virginia. Makes people sick, too."

"Well, is this it?" asked Uncle Joe.

"The problem is, so far, no cases of *Pfisteria* have been found in fresh water. Just in saltwater along the coast."

I set my jaw and nodded. "Yeah, if it was that, Cayenne would be off the hook. But, with this junk, we might have pollution after all. We've got to get on back to town." I gave my uncle a quick hug, and we headed the bikes toward the road. We were silent for a good ways. I'd never ridden my bike this distance before, but the miles seemed to be flying by. Finally, I spoke. "This might be big, huh?"

"Very big," said Sam, nodding. "Assuming the facts are there, the data can be proved, and we don't run out of time before you have to give your apology. I guess anything's possible."

"Great pep talk," I said. "Just great."

CHAPTER 21
READY? NOT

Tuesday after school, I went to Sam's house for a conference call with him and his dad. Mr. Wheeler had taken the water samples up to the university the day before. We were all on the call when we heard Sam's dad smack the desk. "This is so perplexing. These samples are a mess. Last week they were clear. My team up here can't understand the fluctuation between water samples. I'm wondering if there's another variable I'm not seeing."

"I think there might be, sir," I said, softly. "It's called the human one."

Mr. Wheeler said, "Human?"

"Dad, I didn't get to tell you," Sam said. "We saw busloads of workers at the plant this weekend. I just downloaded some pictures Emily took out there this weekend. I'm sending you an e-mail right now with the attachment."

We waited a couple of minutes until Mr. Wheeler had them up on his screen. We knew because he whistled and said, "Tell me about this."

"I took these Sunday. They were working on *Sunday*," I said. "See, when we first came up with the idea of testing the water, I thought the factory was closed on weekends. But if the plant is running and they're working, timing of the samples might be important. I got the idea because my dad has had some bad experiences with weekend crews. He told me they're usually part-time or temp people who don't know what they're doing, and mess things up."

"Hmm, that's interesting. So, these fish kills have only happened on weekends?"

"Well," I said, "right *after* the weekend. At least the ones we know about."

"Wouldn't Buford Craver be aware of, as you put it, things getting 'messed up'?" asked Mr. Wheeler.

"Depends," I said. "Maybe he cares more about how *fast* he can get the clothes made than *how* he gets it done."

"Very perceptive, young lady," said Mr. Wheeler.

"Thanks, but what do I do with it?" I said, in frustration. "I still haven't proved he's killing the fish."

"Proof can come in many forms. You both know I'm not the scientist on my team. I'm the economist, but I finally might be of some help here. These pictures plus the crazy water samples might mean something after all. We academics don't usually say things like this, but keep your fingers crossed. As soon as I know anything, I'll be back in touch. In the meantime, Emily, keep prepping for Friday. Bring your photos, results of water tests, and though I hope you won't need it, your apology."

The next few days whirled by in a blur, with teasing whispers behind my back ("Practicing your kneeling, Em?") and mock apology notes taped to my locker that started like, "S is for sad, 0 is oh, gee, and R is for real dumb." I kept crumpling them up and pitching them in the trash.

Friday after lunch, my guidance counselor pulled me from class, and I spent the afternoon in the library feeling like I was sequestered in the witness protection program. I put the finishing touches on my PowerPoint presentation and headed for the office. A couple of kids motioned me over to them, but before I could cross the hall, I felt a tap on my shoulder. The principal stood there smoothing her tailored suit and checking her watch.

I swallowed, and said, "Hi, Miss Gruen."

"Hello, Emily. Well, it's time. I've come to escort you to the press conference. I hope you've prepared what you're going to say. You're representing the school in a very touchy situation, and a flock of reporters are outside on the front steps."

My mouth fell open. "Press conference on the front steps? I thought it was going to be a little speech in your office."

Miss Gruen nodded solemnly. "I did too. I only agreed to this change because Mr. Craver is a member of the school board. It seems to have grown into quite an event, so now we're letting the technology classes film it to practice their editing skills. Otherwise, it *would* have been a quick meeting in my office."

"Oh, great," I said. "Now, if I tank, we'll have a record of it for all eternity."

Miss Gruen patted my wrist, and said, "You'll be fine. I'll be there. Also, I met your parents. They'll be somewhere in the crowd, on the left hand side, with Mary Carnell and Sam Wheeler."

"Wait, did you say *crowd*?"

Miss Gruen said, "Oh, yes. Mr. Craver let his workers out early and invited people from the community. We got word this morning of what we might be dealing with, so the superintendent of schools told me to be prepared for that possibility."

I nodded, fingering the flash drive in my pocket, and took a deep breath. "I was going to use the computer in your office to project a PowerPoint of my research on the wall." My tiny window of credibility had just gotten shot down, so on to Plan B. "Um, is *Mr.* Wheeler out there?"

The principal shook her head as we moved along the corridor. "I didn't see him."

"Great," I muttered. "Without him, I can see the headlines: 'Middle schooler makes complete fool of herself with lack of evidence.' What do I do?"

"Well, for one thing," said Miss Gruen, "stop twisting your ring so hard. You're going to leave a permanent crease in your finger."

I glanced at my right hand. "Bad habit. I do that when I get nervous. It's my birthstone, for February."

"Ah, you're a Pisces." Miss Gruen nodded, and pointed me toward the door. "No wonder you couldn't give up on those poor fish."

"Maybe that's it," I agreed. "Or I'm crazy."

Miss Gruen frowned. "No one thinks you're crazy, Emily. I'm sorry about not having something set up for your presentation. Just do the best you can, but if you can't prove your allegations, you must proceed with your apology. Please consider your words carefully."

The only words I could think of were "Can we do this some other day?" Before I could speak, Miss Gruen said, "Here we go." She pushed open the door and nudged me into the bright sunlight.

I gasped. A podium draped with the shocking pink logo of Cayenne Textiles stood on the top step. There were only five or six steps leading up to the front door of the school, but they stretched about fifteen feet across. Gobs of people crowded the pavement below, both kids and grownups. Ten-foot wire panels scattered throughout the crowd displayed what looked like every garment the company had ever made. Each wild sweatshirt seemed to be shaking its sleeve at me, as though I were a naughty little girl.

"Wow, look at all those men in suits. Who are they?"

Miss Gruen frowned. "Judging from the briefcases they're holding, I'd say those men are Cayenne lawyers. Those seated folks are members of the board of directors, Mrs. Craver, Cynthia. Of course, you know Cynthia. They have a pretty big entourage. Mr. Craver probably wanted to intimidate you."

Out of the corner of my eye, I saw Cynthia glaring at me. Then, she held her nose, and pointed at me, which I thought seemed kind of juvenile, but then, I wasn't the one sitting with all the VIPs. "Well, I guess his plan worked. I must look pretty dorky," I said, staring down at my well-worn book bag and chewed-off pencil.

"You look just fine," said Mom, appearing beside me with Sam and Mary. "Your dad's about five rows back and has a blue golf shirt on so you can see him. Here's that stuff you asked me to get."

Ms. Gruen motioned for the four of us to move way over to the left side of the top step so we could talk.

"Thanks for bringing this stuff, Mom. As you see, I can't use my PowerPoint." I looked at Sam. "Where's your dad?"

He shook his head. "I tried to call him during lunch, but it went to voice mail."

It was then that my stomach lurched like I'd dropped from the peak of a roller coaster. Without Sam's dad, two choices flashed before me: faint and be carried away on a stretcher or... I couldn't think of the other choice.

"Guess I'm on my own." I reached in the oversized brown envelope and pulled out a number of papers, careful not to turn them toward the crowd. Sam took a few pages and so did Mary. "When I nod, flash these up so everyone can see them." I tucked the envelope under my arm. "Ready or not, I guess this thing is about to start."

A hush fell over the crowd as Mr. Buford T. Craver tapped the microphone with his gold pen. "How are y'all doing today?"

I turned toward the podium so I could see this guy, and muttered, "Mr. Slick."

Mom glanced at the crowd and whispered, "Doesn't matter. He signs lots of their paychecks."

Several people stared at me, including Cynthia. The anger in those eyes made me wish there were more earthquakes in Virginia so I could fall into a crack. Instead, I had to face Cynthia's dad.

Mr. Craver opened his arms wide like he was hugging the crowd. "Thank you so much for coming today." Up close, I saw he was medium height, had short gray hair, and looked like he belonged in a menswear catalog. He wore a crisp, dark blue blazer, white shirt, navy and red striped tie and khaki pants, and he paced excitedly back and forth behind the podium. "Well, my fellow citizens, as many of you know, work is what our company stands for. We work hard to make the best sweatshirts and leisure clothes in the world." He paused for some polite applause. "But someone has been trying to stop our efforts with allegations that we are responsible for destroying the natural habitat of our wonderful local fish population. I assure you fine folks that nothing is further from the truth." He paused again and nodded at three men in suits who proceeded to rush around like a video on fast-forward. They set up easels with complicated-looking graphs and photos of the interior of the plant.

Mr. Craver smiled as if he'd been crowned Mr. America, and went on. "I'm so glad to have this opportunity to set the record straight about the claims of Miss Emily Sanders. We applaud her concern for our beautiful wildlife, but she's wrong about Cayenne Textiles. We've had independent lab studies conducted on both air and water, and as you can see from the charts behind me, all the results are in the normal range for a plant of our size. What's more important is the fact that since I regained control of the company, we have added over one hundred much needed new jobs." He turned to me.

"You're changing the subject, sir," I blurted out. "My complaint was not about employment but about Cayenne Textiles polluting the Higdon River."

"Miss Sanders, we've just shown you our charts. Your complaint is unfounded. Besides, I've been known to cast a line or two in that river. I also love a good trout dinner. Now, don't you have something to say?"

Miss Gruen motioned for him to move away from the podium.

As Mr. Craver shrugged and stepped away, I looked at Mom, Sam, and Mary. I spotted Dad in the audience and he tilted his head as if trying to push me along. All of them gave me the thumbs-up sign. The next thing I knew, I stood at the podium facing a sea of waiting faces. I clutched my notes and the big envelope, and then took another deep breath. "I was born in this county and think it is the prettiest place on earth. The Higdon River, where my Aunt Sylvie and Uncle Joe live, sparkles in the sun, it's so clean and pure. But lately, it hasn't been very pretty. It's gone from this..." I paused, pulling from the envelope a large photograph that showed the shimmering water and a spotless stretch of riverbank... to this." As my friends came forward, they both hoisted large photos in each hand. I pulled out my second photo and jammed it on the podium. Facing the audience, the three of us held close-ups of hundreds of bulging-eyed, bloat-bellied, dead fish. "That's what the river turns into when a company pollutes it. Gross, isn't it?"

The sounds of scraping chairs, grumbling, and random statements like "This kid's no expert," "Who does she think she is?" and "When's the apology start?" circled through the crowd.

"Let her finish," said Miss Gruen.

I took a deep breath and plunged on. "Imagine the worst thing you've ever smelled. A stench so bad you have to hold your nose shut." I stared at the crowd for a moment then gestured to each side of the podium. "These are my friends, Mary Carnell and Sam Wheeler. They believed in what I was doing. Well, maybe not at first, but after they saw the riverbank covered with fish bodies, they helped a bunch. We took water samples up and down the river, at lots of places." Again, our hands raised photographs of the golf course, the boat ramps, the sawmill, and Aunt Sylvie's place. "All the circumstances pointed at Cayenne Textiles, because your company is the only one that needs water to operate. Water where fish live, and *die*."

"Quite true, Ms. Sanders, but water is also vital to a golf course using tons of pesticides each year and a huge component of making lacquer used in furniture finishes." Pointing to all his charts and graphs, Mr. Craver leveled his eyes, gray like charcoal, and unblinking, directly at me. "You may have photos, but you don't have evidence. You have quite a dramatic presentation, young lady, but drama doesn't prove a thing. Don't you agree, Miss Gruen?"

People began to nod and a few clapped in agreement. I looked toward my parents hoping the sight of them wouldn't make tears start dripping down my cheeks. Dad gave me a fatherly nod, and my mom held a finger to her lips like she was blowing me a kiss. They loved me, but they couldn't save me from having to give this apology. I gripped the podium and watched as Mr. Craver stepped forward, grinning from ear to ear. Feeling like I'd never smile again myself, I began. "Mr. Craver, I thought your company, Cayenne Textiles, was doing a very bad thing and somebody should stop you. Everyone can see that things are a mess out on the river, but proof of who was killing the fish was hard to come by. I thought we'd found enough evidence in our last samples to prove who was at fault. I had a PowerPoint to show, but don't have... that is, right now, I can't prove anything. So, that means I have to say... So, um, right now, it doesn't appear that Cayenne..."

Miss Gruen cleared her throat.

I stared at Mr. Craver wanting him to see the determination flashing from my eyes. An apology might be the next thing out of my mouth, but it wasn't what was in my heart. I looked down at my notes, and went on. "I'm sorry to say, it doesn't appear that Cayenne—"

A voice came from the crowd, shouting "Hold everything!" I looked up to see Mr. Wheeler and another man push their way to the podium.

CHAPTER 22
HOOK, LINE, AND SINKER

"Here are your facts," announced Mr. Wheeler, waving a sheaf of papers. He leaped up the steps, handed me the top few papers, and pushed his way to the microphone. "And, actually, Ms. Sanders *had* facts and was so well prepared with a PowerPoint presentation to show them that her teachers would have awarded her extra credit. Unfortunately, she was prevented from showing her presentation by this unexpected change in location. First, let me introduce myself. John Wheeler, father of Sam, and presently on staff as an economist in environmental studies at the University. Emily Sanders came to me with theories, most of them directed at Cayenne, but no proof to back any of them up."

"See?" said Mr. Craver, pointing to the crowd. "I think we can wrap this up."

Mr. Wheeler continued. "However, she kept pushing, or rather *investigating*, and testing the water. Something was killing fish, and, in fact, it turned out to be Cayenne Textiles. The photographs taken by Emily and her family showed us something we hadn't thought of. These hot new colors seen around you today can cause serious problems. Bright color dyes must be diluted properly after the dye process. If this isn't done, when the dyes get to the discharge area, metal particles and other materials..." He paused and pointed to the papers he had handed me.

I held up an enlargement of the water sample Sam and I had gotten Sunday. The junk sparkled in the otherwise clear water in the jar. Mary and Sam fluttered the dead fish photos.

Mr. Wheeler went on. "Metal particles and other materials in such high concentrations pose grave health hazards. Obviously, such damage can occur to fish and turtles. If it goes on long enough, humans can be adversely affected, too."

Several lawyers jumped up and motioned for Mr. Craver to join them. The men huddled together for a few moments then Mr. Craver flashed his smile back on. "John Wheeler here is right, of course, but we corrected our settings a long time ago. None of these recent fish kills are any of our doing."

Mr. Wheeler cleared his throat. "As I mentioned, Emily has quite a number of photographs. Can you share some?"

I nodded and pulled out several enlargements from my envelope. "I took these Sunday at the plant. They show the weekend shift."

A voice in the crowd shouted, "We couldn't hear you in the back. Did you say weekend shift?"

Mr. Wheeler smiled and gestured toward the voice. "Step forward, sir. Tell us your name and where you work."

A lean, muscular man tipped his baseball cap at the audience. "Oscar Smith. I'm an assistant foreman at Cayenne."

"Do you work weekends?" asked Mr. Wheeler.

A murmur rose from the audience. Off to one side, the lawyers and Mr. Craver huddled again. The board of directors sat stone-faced as Oscar Smith replied. "I work whenever the hours are available, but my section was told there wouldn't be any weekend or overtime until after the winter markets."

"Is this true?" asked Mr. Wheeler, turning to the Craver group.

Buford Craver's face turned spaghetti sauce red and started popping sweat beads. "Well, the fact is we had a rush order to get out and didn't have time to call everybody in. Just a one-shot deal. Sorry, folks."

"Emily," said Mr. Wheeler, "do you have one more photo in your folder?"

I drew the last one out with a flourish and plopped it in front of the rest. "This is a picture of the bus the workers came on."

"Hey," said Oscar Smith, "the sign on that bus says Danville Temps. You went out of the county for help? What about us regulars? We'd gladly work some extra hours."

Whispers buzzed through the crowd. A woman in the back said, "Jobs are too precious."

A man I recognized from my neighborhood shouted, "People need work."

Mr. Craver's smile disappeared. He tried to win back the angry crowd. "A one-shot deal, folks."

Mr. Wheeler waved his papers again. "According to Danville Temps, you used their workers six weekends in a six-month period."

Oscar Smith stepped toward the podium. "Is that why our equipment was set wrong Monday when we got to work?"

Mr. Wheeler nodded. "Emily here had a hunch something was going on. I'd say the Cravers saved some money by hiring cheap labor. Trouble is, *inexperienced* help doesn't know how harmful textile dye can be."

Mr. Craver's eyes glowed like coals in a barbecue as he stared a moment at me, then turned and stepped to the microphone. "When I took this company back earlier this year, I underestimated how much had changed in the textile business. This little lady's daddy works for a public utility. *They* get incentives and tax breaks while we in private business have to struggle for every nickel we make."

"You must have a huge pile of nickels somewhere by the look of that corporate jet," a man called out from the middle of the crowd.

Laughs started up, then quickly stopped as Mr. Craver grimly replied, "Sir, you probably don't realize how hard we work and how much we executives travel. We deserve to be comfortable."

The man, dressed in a striped charcoal gray suit, stood up and stood his ground. "Beg your pardon, but I travel for business every week, and a coach seat gets me there just fine. Of course, I don't get a pricey personal chef on board at those prices."

Mr. Craver dismissed the man with a wave of his hand. "As I was saying, competition in manufacturing clothing is fierce. Everything hinges on price."

One of the board members in the front row stood up. "Buford, I want to know why you cut costs to the detriment of the environment. You didn't tell us about this. You knew what was going on was illegal. Weren't there other options? Were there no other ways to make production more efficient?"

"Yes, of course," sputtered Mr. Craver, "but they all would take more time and investment. This was quick, easy, and cheap. I never expected these workers would cause a problem. Who would have thought it would be an issue? Besides, why be so concerned about a few fish?"

The seated members of the audience began to squirm in their seats. People whispered behind their hands to the person beside them. The murmurs swelled like a wave. It appeared the mood of the crowd had shifted.

"People," bellowed Mr. Craver, "does no one hear me? Price, price; if we charge too much we won't sell as much. If we want to stay in business and create those new jobs everyone wants, we need to make money."

"And Daddy has an image to uphold in this community," said Cynthia Craver, jumping up from her seat. Before her mom could haul her back down, she went on. "And that image costs a lot."

Oops, I thought. That girl isn't as bright as some people think.

"Yeah, that image requires that he keep all those race horses and fancy stables," yelled a lady from the sidewalk.

"Don't forget he needs to make money for his big yacht to stay afloat up on Smith Mountain Lake," added an elderly gentleman leaning against one of the Cayenne garment racks.

"And for the antique car collection," muttered Oscar Smith.

With that statement, I thought Mr. Craver seemed to deflate.

Mr. Wheeler cleared his throat and gestured toward the man coming up the steps. "Well, I think we can move along, folks. This is Randolph Hinton, area director of the Environmental Protection Agency. He's here to direct how and what your company needs to do to meet EPA regulations and stay in operation. That is, only after he escorts you to the school conference room to discuss any charges, criminal or otherwise, that are now pending against Cayenne."

"Thank you, John." Mr. Hinton gestured toward me, and said. "This student deserves a big thank-you for getting folks' attention. Up to now, reports about fish dying have been filed, but gotten shoved in a drawer somewhere in Richmond. We're going to find out why. Before too long, thanks to the work of Emily, Sam, and Mary, we will have a hotline for reporting any fish kills around the state. We have a long way to go to prevent this kind of pollution from happening again, but it's a start."

A tall, stately looking lady made her way to the podium. She whispered something to Mr. Wheeler, and he spoke again. "This is Vivian Carson, chairperson of the Cayenne board of directors."

"Hello, everyone. The board is committed to the stability of Cayenne. The trust of the community is important to us. We find with the growth in market share of our new apparel line shown here today, there is no reason our company cannot survive this issue and grow. Proper guidance and management will be the key. As such, an open board meeting will be held at 7:00 p.m. next Monday evening. Workers, shareholders, and community members are all welcome. Mr. Craver's tenure as president will be on the agenda. Thank you."

I stood clutching my dead fish photos as Mr. Craver was guided away, looking as though his team had just lost the World Series. Miss Gruen stepped to the podium. "Emily? We owe you and your friends an apology and a great big thank-you. Come closer, please."

I was so stunned by this crazy turn of events, my feet seemed glued to the steps.

Somehow also, my mom had appeared beside me, and whispered, "Go on, sugar. You won. Be gracious. And Em, you can smile now."

Oh, yeah. And I did smile through the end of the press conference, and later when everyone wanted to shake my hand. I smiled again when the newspapers wanted to take our picture with Mr. Wheeler. But when I left my parents for a minute to run into the school to get something from my locker, I turned off the smile. How do celebrities do that? My face hurt from all that smiling.

As I rounded the hall corner, I ran smack into Leanne. "Hi!"

"Hi," said Leanne, grabbing my arm. "Did you get my messages?"

I nodded. "Yeah, things got kind of crazy recently. I just haven't had time to call you. What did you want?"

"I wanted you to know I'm not friends with Cynthia Craver anymore, and it doesn't have anything to do with fish. Which, by the way, I'm glad you were right about."

"Thanks. So, what's the deal with Cynthia?"

Leanne rolled her eyes. "She's so possessive. Like I'm not supposed to talk to anyone but her. And bossy? You wouldn't believe it. She's always ordering me around. Sometimes I would like to do the ordering."

I nodded. "Yeah, I know. Maybe you're more of a leader than a follower."

"Maybe I am. Kind of like you," Leanne said. "So, will you call me?"

I thought a minute. Having a best, best friend was great because it was nice having someone who knew you through and through. But that person should also be the one who stood by you when things got tough.

"Leanne, remember the day we played tennis, you said you liked change? Well, I decided I like it, too. I've changed a bunch. I'll call you sometime, and we'll talk about it. I'll tell you about the big slumber party I'm planning."

"When?"

I shrugged. "I don't know exactly, but I want you to get to know Mary Carnell, Katie Gilman, and a whole bunch of people. It'll be fun, you'll see." I glanced up to see Mary and Sam heading our way.

As Mary got close, she yelled, "Emily, you did it!" I shook my head as we slapped hands in victory. "*We* did it. You, Sam, and me. And Mr. Wheeler, of course."

"True," agreed Mary, with a shrug. "Hi, Leanne. Sorry to butt in."

"That's okay, I should probably go," said Leanne, looking unsure of what to do next.

"Thanks for coming by," I said. "Like I said, I'll call you."

Leanne nodded. "Sure, my ride is probably waiting for me. See ya, Em."

Before I could reply, Mary blurted, "Guess what? Mr. Chicelli finally wants to put the whole fish thing in the school paper. A special edition. Do you believe it?"

As I watched Leanne go, my feelings tumbled around. She was such a big part of my past, but now probably a part of my new, improved future, too. Things were good. I blinked, and my smile returned. "Wow, it's about time."

"I know," agreed Mary. "So, your mom and dad sent us to get you. They're taking us to Dairy Heaven to celebrate. I'm going to get my stuff. Your mom said for us all to meet in the parking lot."

I nodded as Mary left, then turned to open the locker. I was pawing through heaps of old tests when I heard Sam clear his throat.

"Uh, Emily." Sam scuffed his running shoe on the floor. "I know I gave you a hard time when we first met. But I wanted to tell you what a good job you did about the fish."

"Thanks, but I couldn't have done it without you and your dad."

"Yeah, I *do* have skills," he said, grinning. "And Dad can come through in a pinch. Listen, do you want to eat with us Saturday night?"

I was quiet for a moment. "Uh, will Cynthia be there?"

Sam tossed his shaggy hair. "Cynthia is not an issue for me anymore. She's changed. Or maybe I have."

"You too?" I grabbed what I needed from the locker. "Well, yeah, I guess I could eat at your house. That would be fun."

"Great," said Sam. He started off, and then turned around. "You should wear your hair like that more often. It looks nice."

"Thanks." I rubbed my hair, wondering how many hours it had been since it had been brushed. Okay, it was one thing for my dear aunt or a friend to say I was beautiful. But, no guy, except maybe my grandpa, had ever said anything good about this mop of red curls. Sam's comment gave me a funny feeling inside, kind of fluttery.

"So," said Sam, "I'll catch up with my dad. We'll see you at the ice cream place."

I watched him walk down the hall, thinking I, Emily Sanders, was going to have dinner at a guy's house. What did this mean? Sometimes life seemed like one big quiz show. Just when I think I have all the answers, they throw me a bonus question.

ABOUT THE AUTHOR

Gail E. Hedrick, middle-grade fiction author, freelance writer, editor, proofreader, and former teacher in the physical education field, reads the sports section everyday, loving the stories behind the scores. Spurred to write herself, after her first piece sold, she was hooked. With subjects ranging from how-to's, fitness, and etiquette to mysteries, she is read by kids and teens everywhere. She grew up on a lake in Michigan, spent many years on the lakes and rivers of Virginia and North Carolina, and now lives in Bradenton, Florida, and can be reached at www.gailehedrick.com.

ACKNOWLEDGEMENTS

I am so very thankful to a myriad of helpful people: Patrice and Ed Newnam of Virginia, Elaine Albertson, Carrie Rogers and Penny Noyce of Tumblehome Learning, and my critique group of accomplished children's writers/authors-Joan Hiatt Harlow, June Fiorelli, Carol H. Behrman, Elizabeth Wall, Betty Conard, and Diane Robertson. I am grateful to my writing cheerleader, Aunt Yarda (Ervin), my encouraging cousins and fish folk, Chris Ervin and Tim Ervin, and my tireless first reader, husband, Mont.

MORE SCIENCE FUN IS ON THE HORIZON AT

TUMBLEHOME
learning

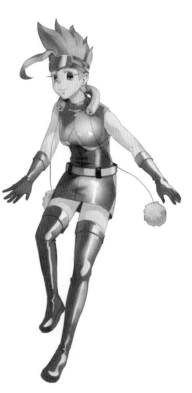

Whether you're interested in engineering, dinosaurs, space, biology, or other wonders of the universe, we have something for you. Check out our website for more Galactic Academy of Science books and other fun and inspiring THL offerings:

www.tumblehomelearning.com

G.A.S. SERIES

CLINTON AND MAE'S MISSIONS:
The Desperate Case of the Diamond Chip
The Vicious Case of the Viral Vaccine
The Baffling Case of the Battered Brain
The Perilous Case of the Zombie Potion

ANITA AND BENSON'S MISSIONS:
The Furious Case of the Fraudulent Fossil
The Harrowing Case of the Hackensack Hacker
AND COMING SOON:
The Confounding Case of the Climate Caper

ELLA AND SHOMARI'S MISSION:
The Cryptic Case of the Coded Fair

... and more G.A.S. adventures on the way!